A KILLER VIEW

A PARKER LEE MYSTERY

M.P. BLACK

1

"What a perfect day," Mom said.

She and I were finishing lunch on the back porch of the Lakeview Inn, my Aunt Lil's boutique hotel, and it really was a perfect day: the sun sent ripples of silver across Lake Allington. Sailboats drifted past Gull Island. A single-prop airplane soared, albatross-like, high overhead.

We were eating a lunch salad with grilled pear, walnuts, and a thick balsamic. Mom finished the last slice of pear on her plate and put down her fork.

"So, Parker," she said, dabbing her mouth with her napkin, "we've talked about my work—what's going on at *The Gazette*?"

I chewed a slice of pear. A burst of charred sweetness. Then swallowed.

"A guy sighted a northern saw-whet owl in the Allington Woods."

"Wait," Mom said. "A real northern saw-whet owl? That's incredible."

I nodded and smiled. Trying to make my smile look

genuine. Spotting a northern saw-whet owl counted as breaking news, and as a journalist at my dad's newspaper, *The Allington Gazette*, it was my job to cover the story. But once in a while, I couldn't help but miss a big, juicy scandal. Or a shocking crime. The kinds I studied at journalism school. The kinds I covered during my brief stint as a reporter at a major national newspaper in the city—before I got laid off and moved back home.

I'd hoped that lunch with mom would've uncovered something interesting. But these days, crime, like everything else in town, was slow. Allington was peaceful. And that was good, wasn't it? That was what we wanted, right?

"What else?" Mom asked. She brushed a fleck of dust from her uniform. Mom's uniform was, as always, neatly pressed. On her chest, the badge that said "Chief" shone. So did the brass name tag with the "C. Lee" engraved on it. Both spotless. She added, "Are you covering Amy's fundraising events?"

"Of course."

My sister Amy was the pastor at Shepherd's Gate Church, and she was running a series of fundraising events this month. Which, of course, *The Gazette* would cover. In the Lee family, we were all about helping each other.

"But to be honest," I added, "I wish I had something more exciting to report."

"You want exciting?" a voice said.

The door to the inn's lounge opened, and Aunt Lil stepped out onto the back porch. She wore a bohemian kaftan that billowed over her legs. A dozen bangles jangled on her wrists, adding to the rattle of the many necklaces she wore.

"A great flood. The water rising. A desperate struggle against time."

"Is this a mythic story?" Mom asked, sounding skeptical. My mom was the rational one. Aunt Lil was the family mystic. "I mean, are you talking real life here, or are you sharing one of your, um, *insights*?"

"My insights are real life," Aunt Lil said. "Anyway, I'm talking about the basement."

"Ah, I see," Mom said, a little smile quirking her lips.

I frowned. "I don't see."

"I'm guessing a pipe burst," Mom said. "In Lil's basement."

"You're guessing right," Aunt Lil said.

She pulled out a chair and sat down, her kaftan coming to rest along with her clattering jewelry. She told us her story with much hand waving and drama: early Thursday morning she had gone down into the dark basement to get a lightbulb—a lamp in one of the rooms upstairs needed a new one—and she'd stepped right into an inch of water.

"My slippers are ruined. But I'm more worried about the damage to the inn. So I called an emergency plumber, of course. He's down there now."

"That's awful," I said.

I didn't add that it hardly qualified as a good article for *The Gazette*. A burst pipe wasn't breaking news. Even our little local newspaper had its standards.

Aunt Lil must've sensed my reticence, though, because she shrugged and said, "Fine. I can tell you don't want my 'Great Lakeview Flood' story. But that's not all." She leaned forward, a frown gathering on her face. "One of my guests has vanished."

Mom and I looked at each other.

"Vanished?" I said.

"Disappeared." Aunt Lil fluttered her hands in the air. "Poof, gone up in smoke."

"You mean," Mom said, her skeptical look returning, "that you actually saw him vanish in a cloud of smoke?"

Aunt Lil snorted. "Of course I'm not saying that, silly. Don't take everything so literally."

I suppressed a smile. Mom could be too literal. But to be fair, Aunt Lil was also likely to say that someone literally vanished in a cloud of smoke.

"He arrived on Tuesday," Aunt Lil continued. "But I haven't seen him since the day before yesterday."

"Maybe he's gone on a long hike, and he's staying at a shelter in the woods," Mom said.

The Allington Woods, which surrounded Lake Allington and our town, stretched far and wide, reaching up into the mountains in the distance. A great place for hiking. And a pretty good place for getting lost, too.

"He paid cash, one day at a time," Aunt Lil said. "Which means his stuff is sitting in that room free of charge."

The door to the inn's lounge opened and Zadie, the Lakeview's housekeeper, stepped onto the deck. She was carrying a mop and a bucket.

"Zadie," Aunt Lil said. "Any sign of the guest in room 9?"

Zadie shook her head. "The do-not-disturb sign is still on the door."

"Strange..."

"But Lil, one of the guests—Mr. Humphries in room 7—he said a sound woke him Thursday night or early Friday morning. When he looked out the window, he saw someone lurking outside on the dock."

"Lurking?"

"That's what he said. But the person must've seen him. Got right into a boat and rowed away."

"Did he see anything else?"

Zadie shook her head. "He said he was half asleep, and

he didn't have time to put on his glasses. He couldn't even tell whether it was a man or a woman. The person wore a cap that hid their face. And he thought a second person might be rowing the boat. Which, he said, might mean it was just someone out fishing. By the time we were done talking, he'd convinced himself that was the explanation." She frowned. "But why would a fisherman stop at our dock?"

"Yeah, that makes no sense. Zadie, thanks for telling me."

Zadie walked down the wraparound porch and turned the corner.

For a moment, Mom, Aunt Lil, and I sat in silence.

Then I said, "He left his stuff?"

Aunt Lil nodded. "And I've got a bad feeling..."

"He'll turn up," Mom said, sounding unconcerned.

But I wasn't convinced. Mom might be reacting more to Aunt Lil's "bad feeling" than the facts. Yes, my aunt could be a little woo-woo, but she sometimes really did have "insights." Plus, she ran a successful hotel. If she was worried about a guest, shouldn't we take that seriously? And wouldn't a missing guest make a good story for *The Gazette*?

"Maybe we should go take a look room 9," I suggested.

Mom sighed. "Not you, too."

But when I got up, she pushed back her chair, too.

Aunt Lil shot to her feet, her jewelry rattling. She opened the door to the lounge, guiding us through the room full of antique furniture and past the gigantic fireplace. Then into the corridor that led to the reception. Up the old Victorian staircase to the floor above.

"Room 9 is right down this way."

We turned into the right corridor, and Aunt Lil came to a dead stop.

Ahead of us, a person in a black bomber jacket and black baseball cap leaned over the door to a room. Fiddling with the lock.

"That's room 9," Aunt Lil said.

"Hey," Mom cried out. "What do you think you're doing?"

The person glanced back at us. Then turned and bolted, sprinting down the corridor. Sneakers padding the thick carpeting.

I cursed. Then broke into a run.

2

The intruder—a man or woman, I couldn't tell—was fast. By the time I reached halfway down the corridor, they'd yanked open the door at the end and vanished from sight.

"Don't let 'em get away," Mom yelled.

She ran right behind me. And judging by the loud jangling of bangles and necklaces, Aunt Lil wasn't far off, either.

I reached the door, pulled it open, and darted into the stairwell. Dark. Too little time to look for a light switch. The railing and the steps were grayish lines in the gloom.

I flew down the stairs, encouraged by the sound of footsteps below.

Halfway down, the lights went on.

Aunt Lil must've hit the switch. As I turned on the landing, I caught a flash of Mom's blue uniform above me as she came barreling downward. I took the steps, three at a time, down toward the bottom.

I stopped.

Two doors—one to the right leading outside, a glowing

"Exit" sign above it, the other back into the old Victorian's warren of corridors.

The door to the left went *snick*.

Mom came bounding down the stairs.

"This way," I said, heading for the door that had closed.

"Hold on," Mom said, and she tapped her gun holster. "I'll head this way. You go outside and keep an eye on things, in case the intruder exits. Deputy Douglas is on his way."

"Mom—"

"Don't argue," she snapped, and she yanked open the door. "Go!"

She vanished inside.

She was right, of course. If this was a criminal, an experienced police officer could handle it best.

I turned around and went to the exit.

Aunt Lil appeared on the stairs, and I quickly explained what was happening. She was breathing heavily—and waved her arms, bangles clattering, gesturing for me to go. "I'll catch up," she said, in between huffs and puffs.

Outside, I stepped onto the wraparound porch. I considered which way would make the most sense to go. The guest in room 7 had seen someone on the dock. Maybe this intruder? So the dock might be the place to go. Was a getaway boat waiting there? Then again, a getaway car would be faster and more reliable in broad daylight.

As I was considering my options, I heard a snap—a twig breaking—off in the woods. I looked up. Steps led down from the porch onto a verge of grass. Beyond that lay the woods. An endless stand of white pines and paper birch, with ferns and rocks scattered along their roots.

And, some distance into the trees, a person running.

My heart leaped into my throat. Black jacket. Black cap.

It was the intruder. The other door closing—that had been a ruse to lead us off the scent.

I broke into a run. I jumped over roots and rocks—and, landing awkwardly in a hole, nearly twisted my foot. Up ahead, the intruder was a distant black shape.

I clenched my fists. You're not getting away from me. You have a head start, but I know these woods well.

I bounded over a rock, and I was skirting a giant tree when a sharp pain dug into my foot, and I cried out. I stopped and dropped to one knee. A root had caught my sneaker. I'd been too distracted by my own thoughts to notice the danger.

Now I looked up, making sure I didn't lose sight of my quarry. And saw the black-clad figure approach a large black shape among the trees.

No.

The intruder vanished into the black shape, an engine revved, and then the car sped off. The vehicle flashed between the trees, following the old logging road.

Then, as the road turned, the car disappeared from sight.

I flexed my foot. It was all right. Nothing broken. My pride was another matter. Seriously bruised.

I dug out my phone and called my mom. While I waited for her to answer, I thought about the intruder. The person had obviously been trying to break into room 9. The room belonging to the missing guest.

What the heck was going on?

3

unt Lil removed the do-not-disturb sign and unlocked the door to room 9. The room was dark, the curtains drawn, and she flicked the light switch.

It was one of the smallest rooms at the inn, with barely enough room for a miniature writing desk, a bedside table, and the bed. The missing man—Rolf Goldman, according to the hotel registry—had left the bed in disarray.

"Looks like he slept here," I said.

"But if he left town," Mom said, "he forgot something."

She pointed to a duffel bag on the chair by the small writing desk.

Nothing else noteworthy in the room. Except...

On the bedside table lay an open Bible, face down.

"You still keep Bibles in your rooms?" I asked. "I thought that was a thing of the past."

Aunt Lil shrugged. "At first, I didn't. My feeling is people can figure out for themselves what—if any—religious texts they want to read. But Bibles keep turning up, anyway. Probably courtesy of the Gideons. So I decided to supplement.

Create some variety. If you call room service, you can get books on Buddhism and astrology and near-death experiences and—wait a minute—" She picked up the Bible. "This isn't one of the Gideons. He must've brought it."

I looked over her shoulder at the open pages. Apparently, the man in room 9 had been reading the Gospel of Luke. He'd circled a passage from the parable of the prodigal son:

And the son said unto him, Father, I have sinned against heaven, and in thy sight, and am no more worthy to be called thy son.

But the father said to his servants, Bring forth the best robe, and put it on him; and put a ring on his hand, and shoes on his feet:

And bring hither the fatted calf, and kill it; and let us eat, and be merry:

For this my son was dead, and is alive again; he was lost, and is found. And they began to be merry.

"Lil," Mom said, her tone sharp. "Put that back where you found it. In fact, both of you—don't touch anything."

Aunt Lil raised an eyebrow. "Why are cops always so commanding?"

"Yeah, cops and big sisters," Mom said with a smile.

Aunt Lil returned her smile. "Well, anyway, little sisters are always pawing things, aren't we?" She nudged me. "Aren't we, Park?"

Despite their differences, Mom and Aunt Lil loved each other. In that way, they reminded me of my relationship with my own siblings. We were all different. We all loved each other.

Aunt Lil was about to put the Bible back on the bedside table, but I stopped her.

"Look what was underneath."

"Oh."

A wallet lay on the bedside table. The open book had covered it.

I stared. So did Aunt Lil. It was a well-worn leather wallet. Not the kind of thing you'd leave behind if you were going on a hike. Aunt Lil saw the guy on Thursday. It was Saturday. That was a long time to go without your wallet.

My stomach tightened. I didn't like this.

I heard a snap behind me, and it made me jump. Mom squeezed past me, as she snapped a latex glove on her other hand, both now protected. She gingerly picked up the wallet and flipped it open. Inside a sleeve was a driver's license. She slipped it out. The photo, rubbed and stained, was difficult to make out, but the name was clear: Rolf Goldman.

Mom carefully put the wallet back where we found it. Then turned to Aunt Lil. "That bad feeling you described, Lil? I've got it now, too."

She wasn't the only one. My gut was one hard knot.

4

The clack-clack of Dad's typewriter echoed in the high-ceilinged offices of *The Allington Gazette*. The former firehouse had lots of air and light, but only two employees: Dad and me. It was like working at a desk in a cathedral. Though without the stained-glass windows. And with a vintage typewriter on each desk. Dad had a thing about analog technology—typewriters, turntables, landline telephones. Even old filing cabinets along the walls. Charmingly retro.

As I scrolled through webpages on my laptop, I ran a hand along the smooth edge of the wooden desk. Years of rubbing had made it glossy. On the surface, ghostly grooves showed where someone had leaned their elbows, year in and year out. This was my great-great-grandmother's desk. She founded *The Allington Gazette* in 1871 as a "journal for the people." Much had changed since then. For one thing, she'd run *The Gazette* from her own home at first. But one thing had remained constant through the decades: the publisher and editor-in-chief had always been a Lee.

Suddenly, I noticed the silence. No more click-clack-clack.

I looked up from my laptop. Dad was staring across his desk—which abutted mine—at me.

"You're not typing," he said.

"I'm not."

He wrote on a teal green Olivetti Studio 44. Mine was a candy red Royal Quiet de Luxe. I used to roll my eyes at his typewriter obsession. Who used typewriters, anyway? But since returning to Allington, I'd come to appreciate how a first draft, banged out on a typewriter, somehow sounded— and *felt*—better.

I said, "I'm researching the missing man at the Lakeview Inn."

"Ah, yes, the mysteriously vanishing hiker."

"If he really did go hiking," I said. "Anyway, he certainly didn't leave a trail on the internet. I've found a few Rolf Goldmans, but no one at or even near his address in California. And no one matching his description."

"Well," Dad said with a shrug, "he'll turn up. And the whole thing may turn out to be a misunderstanding."

"But what about the intruder? And the fact that Rolf Goldman left his wallet behind?"

"It doesn't look promising, I'll admit that. But it's too soon for us to write about this. If the guy's run into trouble, your mom will find him. And when she does, we may have an interesting story on our hands. But until then..." He pointed at my typewriter. "Don't you owe me some articles for tomorrow's edition?"

"Yes, Dad," I said with a sigh.

"And don't you need to prepare for covering your sister Amy's fundraising events this coming week?"

"Yes, Dad."

"And are you just yes'ing me, or can I expect a draft of the northern saw-whet owl article by the end of the day?"

I slipped a fresh piece of paper into my typewriter and hit the carriage return. It made a gratifying ding.

"You'll have it within the hour."

Dad smiled. "That's my girl."

5

My sister Amy's church, Shepherd's Gate, usually drew a good crowd on Sundays, and this Sunday was no different. People filled most pews. The Lees took up a whole row: Scottie on the outside, then Joy, Ray and his wife (Roxie), Mom, me, and Dad.

After leading an initial hymn, Amy welcomed everyone before turning to practical matters. She mentioned the month-long fundraiser, which would culminate in three events this week: a Tuesday movie night, Thursday yoga and meditation, and, finally, Sunday family party after the service.

"Please tell your family, friends, colleagues, and neighbors—the more, the merrier. And if anyone would like to volunteer, please come see me."

Mom nudged me and gave me a look.

"Of course I'll volunteer," I whispered.

Amy began the sermon. She spoke about a Jesus parable in the Gospel of Luke—the one about the lost sheep, and how the shepherd leaves the 99 others to find the one—and I glanced at Mom.

Even though I lived at home—at Broadstairs House, our old Victorian—I'd hardly seen Mom since yesterday. She'd been busy with a complaint at the Lake Allington Resort & Spa and then searching the woods for signs of the "missing hiker." I wondered what she'd discovered.

"I couldn't find anything about Rolf Goldman," I whispered. "How about you?"

Mom put a finger to her lips and gestured toward my sister. I should've expected this. Mom was a stickler for paying attention in church.

I turned to Dad instead. "Hey, Dad—did Mom and Deputy Douglas find anything?"

Dad leaned close. "Nothing," he whispered. "But you know how big the Allington Woods are..."

I nodded. "Anyway, we don't even know if the guy went hiking. Maybe he left town."

"Right. Or maybe he knows someone in town, and he's staying with them."

"But would he leave his wallet behind, then?"

"Shhh," Mom shushed us.

I focused on Amy again. Soon, the sermon was over, and she led the congregation in prayer. Then it was time for communion. Followed by more singing. And finally, Amy blessed us all: "May God bless you, fill you with peace, and help you find the lost sheep in your life."

While Amy shook hands with congregants, the rest of us Lees gathered at the table with refreshments. As usual, we enjoyed coffee, tea, and baked goods courtesy of Cafe Larke, my sister Joy's coffee shop. Even though it was self-service, Joy stood behind the table, making sure people got served.

She did it with her usual smile. Some people assumed Joy was so cheerful because of her yoga practice—in addition to the cafe, she ran the Pure Joy Yoga Studio—but having grown up with her, I knew better. Joy had always been full of joy.

My brother Scottie grabbed a fudge brownie and a cup of coffee. He wore one of his souvenir baseball caps. This one was white and said, "All for Allington" in red letters. Plus, a t-shirt with his business logo: Scottie's Ice Cream Shop. Which was down on the docks near the Lake Breeze Brewery & Restaurant, known to everyone simply as "The Breeze." Ray and Roxie, who owned the Breeze, only stopped by the refreshments table to gulp down some coffee. Then excused themselves—they had to get home to their energetic Dalmatian, Wimsey, who they'd left with a neighbor.

Mom sipped a cup of coffee. Then, before I could talk to her, she turned to a woman with gray hair and rings under her eyes: Marina Kemp, the treasurer of Shepherd's Gate Church. They got talking.

"I'm running the yoga and meditation evening, of course," I overheard Joy tell Scottie and Dad. "And then I'll be serving refreshments at the movie night on Tuesday and the family party on Sunday."

I jumped into the conversation. "Well, I'll be covering the events for *The Gazette*."

"But you'll have time to volunteer, too," Dad said. "Won't you?"

"Uh, sure. Maybe I can handle admin stuff. Like tickets."

"Don't be crazy, Park," Scottie said. "I'm the money guy in the family, the only one with a head for business. I'll handle tickets."

"Oh, no," Marina Kemp cut in. "I'm taking care of the tickets and any donations."

Amy joined us. "Marina, please take advantage of my siblings—they can help us—and I'm sure you've got lots of other work to do."

Marina shook her head. "No." It was a firm no. She repeated: "I'm taking care of the tickets and any donations."

"All right," Amy said with a smile. "Then Scottie and Parker, why don't you two volunteer together on Tuesday for the movie night? You can handle the movie projector and show guests to their seats."

"Great," I muttered. A whole night spent listening to Scottie talk about his latest business ventures and how much money he was going to earn. I couldn't wait. I took a deep breath and let out a sigh, reminding myself this wasn't about me. The fundraiser was a big deal for Amy. I was doing this for her.

Amy turned to Marina. "Can the two of us go over the donations so far? It looked like this week's creative writing workshop and contemplative prayer session were both a hit."

"Well, I wouldn't get your hopes up," Marina said.

Amy was visibly taken aback. "What do you mean?"

Marina was fiddling with a button on her blouse. "We fell short of our goals again."

"Again?" Amy exclaimed. Then turned to everyone with a smile. "Excuse us."

She motioned for Marina to join her in a more private conversation. Everyone else politely turned to their own chatting. But I inched close enough to overhear what Amy and Marina were saying.

"But I was sure—" Amy whispered.

"I know," Marina said. "But it's not my fault, is it?"

"Of course it isn't. I'd never dream of suggesting it was.

But I'm surprised the donations fell short, given how many people have come to the events. That's all."

"I'm surprised, too," Marina mumbled, looking at her button. Then the back of her hand. Anywhere but my sister's eyes. To me, she seemed cagey. What was going on?

"Park," Dad said, and he grabbed my arm, pulling me away before I could hear what Amy or Marina would say next.

My heart sank. I wanted to eavesdrop more. Maybe Dad knew that.

But when I met his gaze, I could see he looked excited about something.

"Great news," he said.

"Mom found Rolf Goldman?"

"No, no." Dad dismissed the idea with an impatient gesture. "We've got an exclusive story. Allington Tours are launching a new aerial tour, and *The Gazette* has been invited to cover it."

"And by *The Gazette*, you mean—"

"Yup." Dad grinned. "Tomorrow morning, Park, you're taking a plane ride."

6

The Allington Tours airplane lifted off the ground. The ground flashed past the window outside. Ahead of us, the runway ended in a line of trees. The Allington Woods. I gripped my seat.

"Here we go," Eric Gilder said as he increased the throttle and pulled on the control yokes.

The plane cleared the tops of the trees and then banked sharply, turning its nose upward. Gravity shoved me back into my seat. My tongue wanted to climb down my throat. Silently, I chanted a mantra to my gut:

Don't. Spew. Don't. Spew. Don't. Spew.

Out the small window of the single-propeller aircraft—a tin can with wings—I glimpsed Allington Tours' long red-roofed hangar, the smaller office building, the short airstrip. Then the cluster of buildings grew smaller, and smaller, and smaller.

Gazing down, I clung to my seat.

Trees whizzed past, then water. Lake Allington. Did I prefer to crash into the water or into the trees? I wasn't sure which was worse. I closed my eyes. Tried not to think of either option.

"Hey."

I opened my eyes.

Eric Gilder was looking at me. He smiled, flashing a set of perfect teeth. He was handsome in a conventional, toothpaste-commercial kinda way: clean-cut and neatly dressed in khakis and a polo shirt with the Allington Tours logo on the chest.

"You're doing great."

"Yeah," I said, giving him a thumbs up. "Great."

Don't. Spew. Don't. Spew. Don't. Spew.

The pilot's seat in the small single-propeller airplane sat to the left and slightly in front of mine. Behind me, the two additional passenger seats were empty. Empty like the air out there. A lot of air out there. Again, I looked down—a long way down—and gripped my seat even tighter.

Eric said, "Nothing like it in the world."

Thanks to our headsets, I could hear him over the roar and rumble of the engine.

"Yeah," I said. "Nothing like it..."

"Relax. It's all easy sailing for hereon. Enjoy it."

I nodded, teeth gritted. I'd assumed I was fine with flying. But obviously size mattered. Somehow, a big Boeing jumbo jet didn't put me on edge like this. Maybe it was how close the Cessna felt to the air outside. But Eric was right. Now that the plane moved steadily through the air, I could relax.

I took a deep breath and straightened up in my seat.

He banked the airplane, the wings tipping, and I gripped the seat again.

"Look down there," he said. "Beautiful, isn't it?"

Despite my desire to squeeze my eyes shut, I looked

down. Lake Allington sparkled in the morning sunshine. White sails floated on the shimmering surface. A speedboat threw up a frothy wake.

He was right. It was beautiful.

I smiled. And craned my neck to see better. Nestled in the woods, the white-roofed Lake Allington Resort & Spa glowed in the bright light, like some kind of mythological temple. We curved away from the resort and I got a good view of the town. The docks. The Breeze. Scottie's Ice Cream. Above that, Peony Lane winding upward, with its quaint shops and cafes and restaurants. And higher up, Chestnut Hill, with the big Victorian mansions, the lush Longfellow Park, and the cypresses rising from the cemetery.

I took another deep breath. I was going to be okay.

We flew over the road in the woods, and I caught sight of a black car moving through the trees. Could that be the getaway car the intruder at the inn had escaped in? But we were too far up. And once again, Eric was turning the plane, so we got a different view of the woods and the lake. The black car was gone.

Besides, how many black cars were there in Allington?

I'd better focus on my work.

"So tell me about the aerial tour," I said to Eric, getting back to business.

"We've run aerial tours before," he replied. "And we'll offer a basic bird's-eye view of Allington and the lake. That's the most inexpensive option. But the new thing is a tailor-made tour of the woods and beyond. Whatever people want. We think it'll be a hit with honeymooners."

I nodded. Brought out my notebook and jotted down a few details:

Standard tour stays the same

Tailor-made tour: a hit with honeymooners?

"Your boat tours are already popular with newlyweds, aren't they?"

Eric nodded. "A big attraction, yes. And not just newly weds. Bachelor parties. Business retreats. Family reunions. You name it. We've done it."

"Everyone loves a boat tour of Lake Allington."

"You said it." Eric grinned. "And now we hope people will say the same thing about our aerial tours."

With a steady grip on the controls, he pointed the plane toward the Allington Woods. A blanket of trees stretched out over hills and peaks, dipping into shadowy valleys before rising again. Then the lake was behind us, and I looked down and the ruins of the old sawmill flashed past, half-hidden among the beeches, pines, and hemlocks.

"If people want," Eric said, "we'll take them around the tallest peaks. Or we'll follow the lake around and take a look at town."

He turned the plane again. A moment later, the silvery waters of Lake Allington spread out beneath us again. He pushed the controls forward, and we dipped, dropping further and further down.

The boats were more than just white sails now, and as we flew over one, a tiny stick figure waved. Eric moved the controls, making the wings tilt to one side, then the other.

"I'm waving back," he explained.

"You love this," I said.

He nodded. "Allington Tours is everything to me. As I see it, my wife Iris and I are the luckiest ducks alive."

Again, I jotted down notes:

Eric + Iris Gilder = finding joy in work

What about Mrs. Gilder?

"And your mom? How involved is she?"

"Oh, Mom is the big boss. Always has been and always will be. Well, until she retires."

I'd done my research ahead of time, of course. Betsy Gilder and her husband Greg founded Allington Tours when she was in her late 20s. Greg died young, leaving her alone with two sons and a fledgling business. But through hard work and tenacity, she made it an enormous success. Or so the story went.

We flew over town. Low enough to see cars and people in more detail. And as we passed over Shepherd's Gate Church, I craned my neck to look. A person was hurrying down the path toward the parking lot. Gray hair. Quick step. Even at this distance, I recognized Marina Kemp. But what was that she was holding in her arms—some kind of bag?

I blinked, and she was gone. Or rather, we were. The plane whizzed over town and back out across the water. I frowned. What was Marina doing? I couldn't help but sense something suspicious about her behavior.

We passed over Gull Island, the small island close to town. Some kids used to call it Snake Island. No snakes out there, as far as I knew. Just trees. More trees. And that old ramshackle cabin.

And a flash of red.

What was that—? A knot in my stomach tightened.

"Eric, can you turn back, please?"

He looked at me, eyebrows raised in a question. "Uh, sure."

As the plane banked, I looked down. The sun flashed in my eyes. I held up a hand to shade my eyes.

There it was again.

A flash of red.

"Can we fly lower over the island?"

"We can," Eric said. "But why?"

"I saw something. And I've got a feeling..."

He turned the plane, and we flew lower, bringing us back over the island. And this time I saw what it was: a body lying on the ground, face down, with a bright red scarf strung around the neck.

7

The Allington Police Department speedboat hit the waves and threw spray at my face. Mom stood at the wheel, guiding us closer and closer to Gull Island. A stone's throw from the island, she slowed the boat, cut the engine, and swerved toward shore. I caught hold of a tree bending over the water and threw a rope over it. Mom dropped the anchor.

Silently, we climbed off the boat and onto the island. The knot in my gut—the one that had formed when I saw the body from the airplane—tightened.

As Mom and I moved across the island, we didn't speak. I glanced at her. Could she feel what I felt? Deep in the gut. Something bad. Something horribly wrong.

We pushed aside branches and brambles. Coming to the clearing by the old, ruined cabin, Mom brushed twigs and burrs off her otherwise pristine uniform.

Ahead of us lay the cabin ruin. Weather and time had lobbed off its roof, and it stood headless in the clearing, its top floor exposed to the sky. Empty cans and other trash littered the area. Teens especially liked to hang out on the island.

"There," I said, spotting the body.

It was a man. He lay at the edge of the clearing. Jeans. Sneakers. White t-shirt. And that bright red scarf around his neck. It was a striking, almost flamboyant touch to his outfit.

"Who do you think he is?" I said. Then answered my question: "It must be Aunt Lil's missing guest, Rolf Goldman."

Mom approached him, crouched down, and checked his pulse. She shook her head. Then touched her radio.

"Deputy," she said. "That 10-55 is a 10-67."

Her radio crackled. Deputy Douglas said, "Oh, no. Who is it?"

"We don't know yet. I'll secure the scene. You contact the coroner and get out to Gull Island ASAP."

After signing off, she turned her attention to the body again. She cocked her head.

"What do you think, Park?"

"I think that's interesting."

I pointed at an object in the brush, about 10 feet away. A black baseball cap.

"His hat?" I suggested.

Mom said, "If it's Rolf Goldman, then neither Lil nor Zadie saw him wearing a baseball cap."

"But the intruder at the inn wore a black cap."

"Yes, there may be a connection."

She motioned for me to come closer, and I joined her, crouching down by the body.

I reached out, pointing. "Look—"

Mom put a hand up. "Don't touch."

"Of course not," I said, irritated. Because she reminded me every time. And because my nerves were so taut, they felt like they could snap. "I was simply pointing out that the neck is almost totally covered by the scarf. But you can still see some discoloration. See?"

She leaned closer. Nodded. "Right you are. Possible strangulation."

The man lay face down, but his head was turned to the side, his right cheek kissing the dirt. He had longish hair that fell down his forehead and into his eyes, obscuring large parts of his features on the left side.

Mom studied him closely. Then frowned.

"Wait a second..."

She stood up and stepped over the body, careful where she placed her feet. On the other side, she turned and crouched down again. She took a pen out of her uniform pocket and used it to the lift the hair off the man's face.

She muttered a curse.

"This isn't Rolf Goldman."

"How can you be sure?"

"Because I know him."

I stared at her. She stared back at me.

"This is Ralph Gilder."

"Gilder? As in—?"

"As in Betsy Gilder's other son."

8

That afternoon, Dad and I were click-clack-clacking on our typewriters when Mom came striding into the old firehouse. We both stopped typing. I swiveled around on my desk chair.

"I informed the next of kin," Mom said as she came closer, and she grimaced.

"It went that well, huh?" Dad said.

"Mrs. Gilder more or less kicked me out. But as your sister Joy would say, we all express emotions in different ways."

"How did Eric Gilder take it?" I asked.

"He was visibly shaken, but he and his wife, Iris, were quick to support Mrs. Gilder. Which only made her angrier." Mom shrugged. "I insisted on returning in an hour or so. The coroner estimates Ralph died sometime on Thursday afternoon or evening. I need to know where they were during that timeframe. I said I'd need a full rundown of their movements. They didn't like that. They don't like talking to cops. In fact, they didn't like it back when Ralph took off with the money jar, either."

"Wait a minute." I leaned back in my chair. "Exactly what happened?"

Dad settled down on the edge of my desk. "This happened while you were at journalism school. Ralph Gilder steals a whole heap of money from the family business and skips town. Ditching his responsibilities to his mom. And worse, abandoning his pregnant girlfriend, too."

"How much money did he steal?"

Dad shrugged. "No idea. Mrs. Gilder wasn't exactly eager to share details with *The Gazette*."

I looked at Mom. She shook her head. "Mrs. Gilder refused to report the theft. So it was never an official crime. So, we had no reason to go after him."

"Was this the first time he caused trouble?" I asked.

"Nope," Mom said. "Ralph was a troublemaker in school and then a troublemaker after school. Ostensibly, he had a job at Allington Tours as a tour guide. But I can't say I ever saw him out on the lake or hiking through the woods with tourists. Somehow, he always managed to manipulate extra tips out of tourists."

"How did Mrs. Gilder feel about that?"

"I don't know. That family's skeletons are mostly kept in the closet."

"Mostly?"

"Well, I remember a public fracas between Mrs. Gilder and the girlfriend's father. This must've been shortly after Ralph skipped town. Down on Peony Lane one Saturday. The girlfriend's father, Barry, he stopped Mrs. Gilder on the street. He badmouthed Ralph, and she blew a fuse. Tensions were running high. And then..."

"And then?"

"And then they weren't. No more confrontations. At least not out in public. Life went on. New gossip captured people's interest and Ralph Gilder became part of history. Funny, isn't it? How quickly people can forget other people?"

"So, why would Ralph Gilder come back now?" I asked.

"Good question," Mom said, and checked her wristwatch. "And that's one of the questions I want to ask the Gilders."

"We," I said. "Questions we want to ask. I'm coming with you."

Mom gave me a skeptical look. "I'd love for you to come, Park. But I don't think Mrs. Gilder is going to like me bringing a reporter from *The Gazette*."

"I'll take my chances."

Mom looked at Dad and he threw up his hands.

"Don't look at me, sweetheart," he said. "Park gets her stubbornness from your side of the family."

Mom swatted Dad's arm playfully. Then turned to me. "All right, then. Let's see what Mrs. Gilder has to say about her prodigal son."

I grinned. "You got it."

9

"Chief Lee," the butler said, crossing the driveway and coming toward us. He had the hint of an English accent, like actors in old Hollywood movies. Not quite American, not quite British. "We've been expecting you, of course."

He was coming from the garage, which had three doors and looked like it could accommodate a fleet of cars. But the mansion itself dwarfed the garage. The Gilders lived in one of the massive Victorians on Chestnut Hill, a legacy of the 19th century logging boom in the area.

"Dave," Mom said, nodding at the butler.

Something passed over his face, ruffling his otherwise perfect professional feathers. He smoothed an invisible wrinkle out of his impeccable black suit. Then turned and gestured toward the entrance.

"Please, follow me," he told us.

As Mom and I followed him, I whispered to her, "Dave?"

"David Carlson," she whispered in response. "Mrs. Gilder's butler and chauffeur. He and I know each other well."

She didn't elaborate, and we'd come to the entrance to the mansion: a set of double doors, one of which the butler-chauffeur opened.

As we passed into a dark interior, he said, "Mrs. Gilder may object to the presence of the press."

"I'll discuss it with Mrs. Gilder," Mom said pointedly.

"Very well."

In the marble-floored entrance hall, we passed walls with the shadowy outlines of framed paintings. Occasionally, the face of a portrait rose out of the darkness and gazed down at us, frowning with stern disapproval.

"Cheerful," I muttered.

From the entrance, we passed into what I guess was called a sitting room, which featured heavy drapes, thick oriental rugs, and enough sofas and armchairs for a football team. Through French doors, we passed into a bright garden. After the gloom inside, the daylight blinded me, and I threw up a hand to cover my eyes.

As my eyes adjusted, I took in the patio and lawn. After resting in the sitting room, the football team could come out here and play a game—the lawn was certainly big enough.

At some distance from a house stood a long table with a white tablecloth. The patio we stood on seemed like a perfectly good place for a table. But the Gilders apparently thought it made more sense to set up lunch out on the grass. Maybe rich people got bored with the usual stuff more quickly than the rest of us.

On the table stood four vases with blood-red roses. Pitchers of freshly squeezed lemonade and cucumber water. Platters with sandwiches cut in triangles. Salads arranged— no doubt by a personal chef—in individual glass bowls. Porcelain plates, silverware, and crystal glasses. Plus, two French coffee presses and cups.

Eric and Iris Gilder sat at one end—close together—and Betsy Gilder at the other. Eric wore the same uniform as earlier in the day: khakis and a polo shirt with the Allington Tours logo on the chest. Iris, too.

In contrast, Mrs. Gilder wore a black cardigan over a gray blouse and a charcoal-gray skirt. A pearl necklace around her neck.

She didn't offer us a seat.

"Well, Chief Lee?" she said, as if she were a stern teacher calling on a pupil. "What have you got to tell us?"

"I was hoping you could tell us some things," Mom said.

"We're not the ones you should be questioning. You ought to be talking to that girl, Ashley Waterston, and her brute of a father."

"I will also be talking to the Waterstons. In fact, I'll be talking to anyone who had a relationship with your son."

Mrs. Gilder harrumphed, as if she wasn't entirely convinced by my mom's response. Then she gestured at me. "I see you brought a sidekick."

"My daughter, Parker."

"I know who your daughter is. I'm surprised you thought it was appropriate to bring a journalist to this rendezvous."

"As a reporter at *The Gazette*, my daughter has access to a lot of helpful information."

"Information about my Ralph?"

"At this stage, no. But she may uncover—"

Mrs. Gilder cut her off. "She's a junior journalist at our local tabloid. I don't want her here." She stared straight at me. "Young lady, you can wait by the house for your mommy to finish her work."

My face grew hot. How dare she talk to me like that?

But when I glanced at Mom, she only nodded at me,

acknowledging that Mrs. Gilder had a right to send me away.

"Fine," I said, and spun around and stomped back up to the patio.

Behind me, I heard Mom say, "Now, Mrs. Gilder, I have some questions..."

What I wouldn't give to be part of that conversation. I stopped at the patio. Dave, the butler, was standing there.

"I see we've both been banished," I said.

"This is my job," he said primly.

I shrugged. "This is my job, too."

Down the lawn, Mom was still standing by the table talking to Mrs. Gilder and her son and her daughter-in-law. Clearly, Mrs. Gilder hadn't offered Mom a seat.

"What's Mrs. Gilder like to work for?" I asked Dave.

"She's an excellent employer," he said. Then added, "Not that I discuss such matters with strangers."

"You're her butler and chauffeur, right?"

"That's correct."

"She can't afford a butler and a chauffeur, so she combines the roles?"

Dave gave me a sharp look. "She has no trouble affording staff. She prefers it. She doesn't want a whole army of servants."

Judging by how he said "army of servants," I guessed he was echoing Mrs. Gilder's precise words.

"I get it," I said. "She likes a more cozy setup. Like a family."

"She is very good to us on staff," Dave said, nodding.

I wondered about that. Mrs. Gilder didn't make a good impression on me. Not exactly warm and fuzzy. Did she really treat her staff like family? I would've guessed she was more likely to treat her family like staff.

"And you drive her everywhere?" I asked.

"Everywhere."

"I bet I've seen you drive her around town. Like on Thursday, right? Didn't I see you parking in the municipal lot by the docks?"

"I don't use the municipal lot for Mrs. Gilder's cars," he sniffed, clearly offended by the idea. "Besides, it couldn't have been me you saw, because I wasn't working last week."

"Oh, no—you were sick? I'm sorry. You still look a little pale."

"I'm fine—and I wasn't sick," he said, visibly irritated. "In fact, I took a brief vacation. Mrs. Gilder gave me the week off."

"You went to the Bahamas?"

"I visited family down south."

"South of England?"

He frowned, looking me over as if to gauge whether I was teasing. Which I was.

"No," he said, and his accent slipped a little more. "I'm from here. From Allington."

I tried hard not to smile. So the accent was fake. An affectation. He probably thought it made him more butler-like to sound like Katherine Hepburn.

"Well," I said. "If you weren't here on Thursday, then I guess you can't tell me about Mrs. Gilder's movements on that day."

He stared at me. "Thursday? She was—" He fumbled his words. "She would've been—I mean, I can guarantee she was home. Right here at the house."

"You can guarantee it," I said. "But you can't corroborate it. Is that it?"

He turned away from me, straightening his back and staring straight ahead with a stiff gaze. Ignoring me. He'd realized that, all along, my teasing questions had been a way to get information. He'd remembered that I was a journalist. Below that rigid pose, he would be kicking himself for even exchanging a single word with me.

I didn't feel too bad. I was too busy considering this new piece of information. Mrs. Gilder had given her butler, a key person on her barebones staff, the week off. The very week her prodigal son returned to Allington.

Prodigal son. Funny, that was the passage we'd found in the Bible in Ralph's room at the inn.

Down the lawn, I watched Mom talking to Mrs. Gilder, Eric Gilder, and Iris Gilder. But Mrs. Gilder seemed distracted. She looked up at the house. Her gaze rested somewhere above my head. Or so it seemed. She seemed to be waving something away. A bee?

No, it was an insistent wave of the hand, a gesture, as if she was signaling to someone.

I glanced over at Dave. But he was gone. He must've gone inside without my noticing. So I turned and gazed up at the mansion behind me, trying to see what Mrs. Gilder was looking at.

There. Second floor. In one of the windows. The curtain moved, someone drawing it shut.

Dave? No. Only by sprinting could he have reached the second floor so quickly.

I looked back at Mrs. Gilder. She seemed to be focused on Mom again.

Above me, the window curtain was still. If it wasn't Dave, then who disturbed the curtains at that window? And why was Mrs. Gilder signaling to the person?

I frowned. Mrs. Gilder was hiding something. Or someone.

10

In the bright sunshine the next morning, the Waterstons' ranch-style home looked cheerful. Window boxes overflowed with purple and pink petunias. A dried lavender wreath festooned the front door.

"Quaint," I said.

Mom knocked on the front door. "Snug compared with the Gilder mansion."

"Everything's snug compared with the Gilder mansion."

I looked around. A white van filled the small driveway. Not room for much else. A sliver of lawn. A flowerbed that stuck close to the house. From where we stood, I could almost reach out and touch the hedge separating the property from the neighbor's. A narrow passage squeezed between the hedge and the house. Probably leading to a backyard.

The door cracked open. No butler. Instead, Barry Waterston filled the doorway.

"If you have questions about that worm," he said, barring entry, "you can ask me. Ashley stays out of this."

"Morning, Barry," Mom said.

From behind Barry, someone put a hand on his shoulder. It was Ashley.

"Dad," she said. "It's all right. They need to talk to me."

"They don't—"

"I want to talk to them. Now, let them inside."

Barry grumbled something. But he turned and lumbered down the hallway. Ashley gave us a weak smile as she welcomed us into the home she shared with her father. I knew Ashley from my sister Joy's cafe, Cafe Larke on Peony Lane. Always cheerful. Always asking, "So, what can I get you?" with a big smile—as if the question itself made her happy. Now the smile had faded to almost nothing. Her eyes puffy and red. Makeup smeared.

In the kitchen, Barry walked around the table. The man Mrs. Gilder had called a "brute." Mid- to late 60s. Thick, white mustache. Blue-collar work overalls with smears of oil or some other blackish substance. He walked with a heavy tread, his safety shoes leaving ghostly imprints on the linoleum. Vanishing an instant later.

"Sit, sweetheart," he said, his deep voice rumbling in his chest. Like a bear. He laid a gentle paw on his daughter's shoulder and made her sit.

Ashley wove her fingers around a cup of tea in front of her. She hunched over the table.

A girl of about 4 or 5 years old sat at the table, too, putting together blocks to make a little house. A bowl of oatmeal stood next to her, mostly finished. And a glass of juice as well.

She gazed with big eyes at Mom's police uniform.

Mom said, "Ashley, I have some questions. Questions about Ralph. And your whereabouts on Thursday afternoon and evening. You, too, Barry."

Barry said, "I was working."

"Where exactly?"

He shrugged. "Half of Allington pays me to fix their plumbing. I was driving around in the afternoon. Probably visited half a dozen clients."

"Do you have a record?"

"Right here." He tapped his head with a finger. "I keep my record here."

"He's hopeless," Ashley said. "I tell him to get a computer or a smartphone and keep track of things."

"Is that your badge?" the little girl asked, pointing to Mom's chest.

"Ariel," Ashley said, "Momma and Grandpa have to talk to Chief Lee."

"Momma, Momma," Ariel said, breathlessly, pointing at my mom's holster, "is that a gun? A real one?" Then, before an answer came, she turned to me, "You're not police."

"No, I'm not," I said. "I'm a journalist. You know what a journalist is?"

"I have a journal," she said. Then cocked her head and gave me a serious look, as if she were challenging me. "It's got glitter hearts on it. Wanna see?"

"Ariel..." Ashley said with a sigh.

"Ariel and I'll be out in the yard," Barry said.

"Thanks, Dad," she muttered.

"Come on, Princess. Let's play before we go to your preschool."

Ariel let out a "yay!" and slipped off the chair, racing out the door to be the first in the backyard. Her blocks left behind.

The screen door slammed. Outside, Ariel's laughter filled the air. Inside, her absence left a big silence, only broken by the hum of the old refrigerator.

Ashley pushed herself out of her chair. It looked painful,

but she did it, and then she said, "What would you like—coffee, tea, water? I have sodas, too. And beer. But I guess you don't drink beer."

"Not this early," I said.

"And not on duty," Mom said. "But thanks, Ashley."

I went around the table and touched Ashley's shoulder. Just like Barry had. A gentle hint for her to sit down. "Point me to the tea, and I'll make more for you."

She nodded at a cupboard. Then sank back onto her chair.

Inside the cupboard, I found jars of loose-leaf tea, each neatly labeled. As I doled some into a polka-dotted pot, Ashley said, "I get a deal on tea. From Cafe Larke. That's why I have so much fancy tea..."

Was she apologizing? Was she used to people judging her for spending on luxuries? I'd seen that before. Someone scraping by who felt they had to justify why they had nice things.

This TV was on sale—we got it for nothing. This dress was a present, otherwise I wouldn't—

Mom said, "I'd like to talk to you about Ralph."

"Please, sit," Ashley said.

Mom sat down. I brought over the teapot and two extra cups. I moved a tool belt with wrenches and pipe cutters and other gear from the chair. Barry's stuff, I guessed. Then I sat down, too.

For a while, none of us spoke. The fridge hummed. Outside, Ariel laughed a high-pitched laugh. She yelled, "Graaaaampa!" Delight. Joy. And clearly love.

I said, "They get along."

A weak smile broke the stillness on Ashley's face. "Like a house on fire."

I poured us all three a cup of tea. Then stirred some

honey into mine. Mom blew on hers, but didn't drink. She said, "Ashley, tell us about Ralph's visit."

"It was Wednesday." Ashley choked up. She cleared her throat. Ran the back of her right hand across her eyes. The other hand still clutching the tea cup. "I came home from work and he was waiting at the door."

"Your dad—was he here?"

"He came later."

"What did Ralph say to you?"

Ashley let out a long sigh. "He told me he was a changed man. Things had changed. That he regretted leaving me and Ariel. He said he knew he wasn't worthy of forgiveness—not worthy of being my partner. Said he'd hit rock bottom, but now he was on his way up. That's how he put it. 'On my way up.' He just needed to put his ducks in a row, and if I could give him a second chance, then he'd come back home to me and—" She stopped herself. Once again, choking up. But she recovered quicker this time. "Me and Ariel."

"Did you believe him?"

Ashley stared down at the table. At her cup. "He ran away because of his family, not me. That's what he told me. 'I escaped the clutches of my dear mother once—I'm not doing it a second time.'"

"In the 5 years he'd been gone, did he ever try to contact you?"

She bit her lip and shook her head. She looked back up at my mom and then over at me. Big, doe eyes. Tears ran down her cheeks. She gazed down into her cup again.

Mom said, "Where were you on Thursday afternoon and evening?"

"At work," Ashley said. "Then I picked up Ariel from preschool and we came back home. Dad came home. We all had dinner. I put Ariel to bed. We watched some TV. Then

Dad and I went to bed. It was an ordinary day." Then she added. "For us." And more tears streaked down her face.

Mom had more questions. But I'd heard enough for now. I got up. I pushed open the screen door to the backyard. A stamp-sized lawn compared with the Gilders' football field. But Ariel looked happy. Squealing. Running across the grass. Her granddad lumbering after her with a sprayer bottle.

I joined him, offering to take the sprayer. He handed it over. Breathing heavily. But a smile on his face as he watched Ariel cavort across the grass.

Love. There was love here.

I sprayed Ariel, and she laughed. "Can't soak me, can't soak me," she chanted, running circles around us. "Can't soak me!"

"Oh, yeah?"

I sprayed her, and she squealed. "Again," she cried. "Again!"

Barry and I stood side-by-side. When Ariel ran off to grab another water toy, I glanced over at him. "Did you see Ralph when he was here?"

He nodded. Still staring in Ariel's direction.

"You think he was coming back to stay?"

Barry winced. "Maybe."

"Did Ashley think he was coming home to her and Ariel?"

Barry gave me a long look. Then said, "She's smarter than that."

"She seems pretty upset."

"He was Ariel's dad. He ran out on both of them." He glared at me. "How would you feel if your ex-boyfriend who'd abandoned you with a kid suddenly turned up again? You think you'd be all smiles?"

His words felt like an attack. But they were fair. If I'd been in Ashley's shoes, and my good-for-nothing ex had turned up, and then come to a sticky end, my feelings would've been complicated, too.

"So, why did Ralph come back?"

"What do you think? Money, of course. He'd run out of money. He came back to get more."

"You know this for a fact?"

"I know this for a fact."

Something in his voice...

"Barry, did he ask you for money?"

He nodded. "I planned to pay him, too. Even went to the bank and got out a bundle of cash. I didn't mind. It's only money, and if paying him kept him away from my daughter and granddaughter..." He took a deep breath and then let it out. "I warned the Gilders that Ralph would be back for more money. Though that Mrs. Gilder wouldn't tolerate any criticism of her boy. I bet she welcomed him back with open arms. The poor, foolish woman."

I glanced at Barry. "Sounds like you pity her."

He stared at Ariel as she played, a sudden sadness in his eyes. He said, "Everyone's been hurt by Ralph Gilder. Just in different ways. Maybe we all deserve a little pity."

11

That afternoon, I headed back to the Lakeview Inn, hoping to get more information out of Aunt Lil. I entered the reception. Empty. I dinged the bell and waited.

Meanwhile, I considered the details Mom and I had amassed so far.

Who could've lured Ralph to Gull Island and murdered him there? Ashley Waterston had an alibi. Her dad did, too, at least for the evening. As Mom pointed out, his vagueness about the clients he'd visited Thursday afternoon could be absentmindedness (Ashley said so) or it could be suspicious. I reminded her that no one could corroborate Mrs. Gilder's alibi at all—at least not until the evening when Eric and Iris Gilder joined her for dinner. And then there were those two: Eric and Iris. A dozen people had seen them around town in the afternoon, including Aunt Lil and Zadie, her housekeeper.

I dinged the bell again. Where was everyone? Maybe new guests had arrived and Aunt Lil was helping them get settled.

I climbed the stairs and looked down the corridors. When I got to the second floor, I spotted Aunt Lil, Zadie, and—to my surprise—Iris Gilder standing by a door. Aunt Lil was locking it.

"Thanks so much," Iris said. "And I'm sorry again for being such a pain."

"You're not a pain, Iris," Zadie said.

"Of course you'd say that."

"Well, I say it, too," Aunt Lil said. "You're welcome to check out rooms any time. And I hope the one you picked works well for your dad."

Iris gazed down at her feet. "I hope so, too…"

Zadie put an arm around Iris's shoulders. "Your dad's coming to visit. No matter what happens, that's huge progress. A month ago, the two of you were hardly talking. So give yourself a break. Just take it one step at a time."

"Zadie," Iris said. "What would I do without you?"

Zadie beamed at her. "I'm with you every step of the way. In Allington, we help each other out. Don't we, Lil?"

"That's the truth," Aunt Lil said. Then she saw me and raised an eyebrow. "Park, are you sneaking up on us?"

"I wanted to talk to you, Aunt Lil."

Zadie said, "I'll walk Iris out."

Zadie and Iris passed down the corridor and headed down the stairs, leaving me alone with Aunt Lil. I explained that I wanted to learn more about Ralph Gilder's movements in the time before his death.

"And maybe if the room is open…"

"You want to take another look at room 9?"

I nodded. Aunt Lil shrugged, her jewelry jangling. "I don't see why not. Just don't tell your mom." Then she smiled. "Or tell her. I love it when she gets uptight about procedure."

I tried to convince Aunt Lil that Mom was only uptight about procedure if it didn't involve family, but the two sisters had spent their lives teasing each other about chaos and disorder—I wasn't about to change that.

Aunt Lil led me down to the floor below. She unlocked room 9, and we stepped inside. The bag, the Bible, the wallet—even the sheets on the bed—were gone. Forensics had taken them for testing. So the room looked bare.

As I looked around, I asked Aunt Lil questions about her guest.

"The truth is, Park, I know next to nothing," she said. "I saw him when he arrived, and maybe a couple of times around the inn. But he kept to himself."

"I saw him," Zadie said, coming into the room. She smiled. "Thought I might find you here."

"You saw Ralph Gilder?"

She nodded. "Of course, I thought he was Rolf Goldman. On Wednesday morning—it was early, probably around 7 am—I bumped into him on the porch. He was coming around from the back. Obviously on his way into town. I asked Lil about who he was, and based on my description, Lil said he was the new guest in room 9."

"He must've been on his way to see Ashley Waterston," I said. "Did you see him again the next day, Thursday?"

Zadie shook her head. So did Aunt Lil.

"Who did you see that day?" I asked.

"Jeez, Park," Aunt Lil said. "That could be a long list. And it would include a few guests who've left town by now. But let me think..." She frowned, apparently trying to remember. "Iris Gilder came to see a room, didn't she, Zadie?"

Zadie nodded. "We showed her a bunch of rooms, and then she went home with Eric."

"So Eric was at the inn, too?"

"He'd been in town—on Peony Lane—and came to pick her up."

"What about Ashley?"

Aunt Lil shook her head. So did Zadie. But something flickered in her gaze, and she blinked.

"Zadie?"

"Like I told you," she said, "I didn't see Ashley."

She met my eyes. Even so, she was oddly stiff. Was it something about Ashley? Obviously, Zadie was friends with Iris. Could it be that the Gilders had poisoned Zadie's feelings toward Ashley? Because of Mrs. Gilder's tensions with the Waterstons?

I walked around the bed. The floor was clean. Nothing left over after forensics had gone over everything. I crouched down and peered under the bed. Nothing, of course.

Staring at the nothingness under the bed, I wondered again why Ralph had left all his stuff behind. Something— or rather, someone—had convinced him to leave his room and go out to Gull Island, where he was murdered. That person must've been pretty convincing. What could lure Ralph out to the island? Money, of course.

The killer must also have been sneaky. Because Ralph was not seen leaving the inn with anyone. Could the two of them have gone to the island much earlier in the day, before most people in town were awake? Maybe. But the coroner put the time of death sometime later that day. If Ralph and the killer went to the island in the morning, why wait so long to strangle Ralph out on the island? And if they left in the evening, they'd have to wait until it was pretty dark before they could get to Gull Island without being seen.

I shook my head. The case was still a muddle.

Still crouching, I turned to get up. And saw something. Beyond the foot of the bed, next to the tiny desk, there was a mark on the wall. It wasn't much. Just an indentation. A dent. But from what? A kick? The mark was so close to the floor and almost hidden by the curtains that it hardly seemed like a logical place to kick a wall.

Anyway, this was grasping at straws. The old Victorian inn was probably riddled with dents.

"Found anything?" Aunt Lil asked.

She and Zadie look at me.

I sighed and straightened up, shaking my head.

"Nah. Nothing."

12

By the time I got to Shepherd's Gate Church for that evening's movie night, my brother Scottie had already set up the giant projection screen in front of the altar.

"You're late," he said.

"Sorry," I said. "How can I help?"

"We're mostly ready for the doors to open."

"Maybe I should do ticket sales?"

Scottie snorted, pushed his baseball cap back on his head, and gestured toward the entrance.

"Good luck with that plan, Park. I already asked Marina if I could help and she snapped at me. She's pretty high-strung, that one."

I looked toward the front. A table stood by the arched entrance, near the closed doors. Marina Kemp sat on a chair behind the table. As I headed toward her—ignoring my brother's warning—I noticed a box with a money tray, obviously for the ticket sales. Next to that, Marina had put the collection box: a plain, tall metal container with a slit at the top for money.

She lifted a paper cup of coffee to her lips and drained it.

"Hi, Marina," I said. "Need any help?"

"No," she said, putting down the cup. The dark rings under her eyes looked worse than ever. "I already told your brother. I'll handle this."

"Great," I said, trying to sound cheerful. "I see you've got the collection box out, too."

"Tickets are a flat rate, but people are free to donate, too."

"Do we expect a lot of donations?"

"*We* shouldn't get our hopes up. Let's just hope enough people turn up for us to break even on ticket sales."

Amy came hurrying down the aisle, her robes billowing. She was smiling.

"Here we go," she said. "I'm opening the doors."

I helped her open the double doors to the church, and guests began filing inside. Suddenly, the chatter of happy people rose to the rafters. I glanced out the entrance. A line had formed. More and more people were turning up. This looked promising.

As people paid for their tickets, a few of them dropped money into the collection box. One guy held out a $50 and Marina received it with a smile. She glanced at me and Amy.

Amy gave Marina a thumbs up.

Marina smiled—or tried to. It was more of a grimace. She stuffed the $50 bill into the collection box and turned to the next person buying a ticket.

I leaned close to Amy. "Marina seems so negative about the fundraiser."

"Oh, she's probably just nervous. The last event didn't do as well as we'd hoped."

"Did Marina handle the money for that event, too?"

Amy gave me a look—an arched eyebrow. "Parker Lee, what is that supposed to imply?"

"Nothing," I said. "Unless you want me to imply something?"

"I want you to remember that Marina has served Shepherd's Gate for many, many years, and I trust her completely with her task."

Amy got busy welcoming people. She'd made it clear that Marina was above suspicion. But that didn't mean she was above *my* suspicion. So I kept an eye on Marina.

More people brought money. A woman handed Marina a $100 bill. Another gave her a wad of cash. I was surprised —even thrilled—to see how generous people were. With every gift, Marina stuffed the cash into the donation box.

I was hoping I could take a peek in that box. It would give me a sense of how much money the church was amassing at this movie night. But Marina was glued to her chair, and occasionally she cast me a wary glance. As if she didn't like me hovering near her. How could I get her to leave her station, even for just a few minutes?

Then I had an idea.

Scottie was manning a refreshments table near the projection screen. He was handing a man and a woman each their can of soda and bag of potato chips.

"Soda? Chips?" he asked me.

"Coffee, please."

I returned to Marina with a cup of coffee.

"Thought you could use this," I whispered, as another guest paid Marina for two tickets.

"Oh," she said. "Thank you, Parker."

I stepped back, trying not to look like I was lingering and doing nothing. I waited. More and more people were pouring into the church. The pews were filling. And soon, Marina had finished her coffee.

Before she's taken the last sip, I was back at her side with another cup.

"Here," I whispered, like a little devil on her shoulder, "drink this. It'll perk you up. And I brought you some water, too."

Marina thanked me, took a swig of water, and then another gulp of coffee.

I was planning on getting a third coffee when she waved at me to come over.

"Parker, will you do me a favor?"

"Uh, sure. If I can."

"Just keep an eye on things while I run to the restroom, will you?"

"You can count on me."

Marina hurried off, moving with the quick, frantic steps of someone whose bladder has reached the bursting point.

My plan had worked. A few more guests bought tickets. A guy handed me two $20 bills, and I stuffed them into the collection box. I waited for a gap in the flow of people. The line thinned for a moment, and I leaned forward to look out. Outside the church, more people were arriving.

It was now or never.

I grabbed the top of the collection box and tried to pry it open.

It didn't budge.

But something clanked on the other side.

I turned it around. A padlock. The box was padlocked.

13

For the rest of the evening, Marina stuck to the donation box like glue. All the caffeine I'd fed her only made her more jittery, and when I asked if I could help her with anything, she growled at me: "Didn't I tell you I've got this under control?" Then, to my surprise, her eyes filled with tears. "Why do I have to keep telling everyone?"

After the evening was over, Scottie offered me a ride back to Broadstairs House in the bucket of his cargo bike. I declined. Even though it was late, I wanted to go for a walk, get some fresh air. That's what I told him. In reality, I was heading to *The Gazette*. I wouldn't be able to sleep anyway, not until I learned more about Marina Kemp. Whatever she was up to, she had Amy completely hoodwinked, and it was my job to uncover the truth.

I passed Mo's Convenience Store on the corner and turned into the street where the old firehouse lay, and I stopped.

What was that light? For an instant, I thought I'd seen light streak the tall windows. I stared at the darkened brick building. Then a cone of light swept over the glass again. A flashlight. Someone was inside *The Gazette*.

I ran to the entrance and dug out my keys. But the door stood ajar. Someone had managed to open it. Lock picking. Inside the door, the security alarm panel glowed. I cursed it silently. Dad had installed it after much nudging from Mom, but he'd never activated it. According to him, the panel itself acted as a deterrent. Clearly, he'd been wrong.

I slipped down the corridor to the door leading into the main space. I pushed it open. A couple of paces from me stood a filing cabinet, the first in a row. A person in dark clothes leaned over an open drawer, riffling through manila folders. Black bomber jacket. Black baseball cap.

The intruder from the inn.

"Hey!"

She looked up. Yes, it was a woman. But that little flash of insight was all I got before she grabbed the edges of the filing cabinet and yanked it forward. She danced away as it fell like timber. It slammed against the floor. She bolted.

I pushed open the door, but the downed cabinet caught it. She'd toppled the cabinet to block the door and slow me down.

Well, it worked.

I cursed. Then squeezed through the narrow gap, clambered over the filing cabinet, and then set off in pursuit.

Man, she was fast. Varsity sprinter material. The intruder was down at the other end already, opening the exit door and looking back at me. Was that a smile? The little rat!

I broke into as fast a run as I could manage. She slipped through the door. I reached it a moment later. I grabbed the handle and yanked. But the door didn't budge. I pulled. It rattled in its frame, but something was keeping it shut.

She'd wedged something in the door to seal it. But the stairwell she'd entered would ultimately take her to the street again.

So I spun around. I sprinted back through the long firehouse, climbed over the filing cabinet, and squeezed through the gap in the door. Then hurried to the entrance, which I flung open.

Just as I ran into the street, the dark-clad intruder slipped into a black car. The taillights flared red. The tires screeched, and the car shot forward.

I dug out my phone and rapid-fire snapped as many photos as I could. Then pocketed my phone and dashed after the car.

But the car flew down the street and then careened around the corner. At the corner, a man with a brown paper bag clutched in his hand let out a yelp of surprise.

I ran to his side.

"Guy almost hit me," he said. "Darn drunk drivers."

He took a swig of his bottle. Which clearly wasn't soda. He reeked of alcohol.

Down the street, the car had already vanished. Too fast for me even to keep an eye on, let alone run after. I stood there outside Mo's Convenience Store, trying to catch my breath.

"Did you see the driver?" I asked the drunk with the brown paper bag.

He shook his head. "Dark tinted windows."

I dug out my phone. I stared at the photos I'd shot on my phone, swiping through them again and again. One was blurrier than the next. Impossible to read the license plate.

I let out a volley of curses.

"Whoa," the drunk said. "Some of us don't appreciate cussing."

"I tried taking a photo," I explained. "But totally failed."

The drunk was looking over my shoulder at the photos.

"Aw, too bad," he said.

"Yeah, too bad," I agreed.

"But maybe you can ask Mo if his camera got anything?"

He gestured at something above us. I looked up.

Two security cameras. One pointing toward the fire-house, the other down the street the car had taken to escape. I broke into a grin. Gotcha.

14

The next morning, while Deputy Douglas spoke with Mo about his security cameras, Mom and I visited Cafe Larke to talk to Ashley about the black Mercedes. Inside Cafe Larke, only a few people stopped to sit. Most were in line to get a coffee to go, and maybe indulge in one of Joy's sinfully delicious brownies or muffins.

At the counter, we showed Ashley my least grainy photo of the car.

She shook her head. "I don't know anyone who drives a fancy car like that."

"Thought that might be the case," Mom said.

"Anything else I can help you with, Chief Lee?"

Mom and I exchanged glances, agreeing silently on the plan.

"Two lattes to go and two bran muffins, please."

Ashley smiled. "You got it."

We stepped into the street again, and I climbed into Mom's cruiser. For a moment, we sipped our coffees and nibbled our muffins. Then Mom handed me her bag with the remains of her muffin and put her cup in the cup holder. She switched on the engine.

"Where to next?"

"Eric and Iris Gilder?" I said. "They live on Chestnut Hill. I bet they know lots of people who drive a Mercedes."

Fifteen minutes later, we pulled into the parking lot by Allington Tours. The tour center, with its aircraft hangar and docks for boats, lay on the outskirts of town. This early —and outside of high tourist season—only two vehicles stood parked in the lot: a Tesla and a van. On the side of the van, it said, "Waterston Plumbing."

"I guess Barry's here," I said.

"Great," Mom said, unbuckling her seatbelt. "We'll kill two birds with one stone."

We found Barry first. He was working under a sink in a small addition to the main Allington Tours building. The door was wide open, and on the steps stood a toolbox.

He got straightened up when Mom called his name. He explained that he was installing a new restroom for Allington Tours.

"Took me a while," he said. "But it's almost done. Anyway, you didn't come to talk about my work, did you?"

"We want to ask you about a car," I explained.

"I'm a plumber," he said. "Not a mechanic."

But when I held out my phone with the photo of the black Mercedes, he leaned close to look. He squinted, then shook his head.

"I make good money as a plumber. But not that good."

"But do you know anyone who drives a black Mercedes?" Mom asked.

He shrugged. "Check with the rich folks on Chestnut Hill. I bet you'll find a few Mercedes owners."

Mom thanked him, and we headed toward the main

building to find Eric and Iris. As Mom led the way into the building, I happened to glance back and see that Barry still stood in the doorway to the restroom, staring at us. A deep frown on his face.

We found Iris sitting at a desk, typing on a computer. She shot to her feet, a smile on her face.

"Chief Lee," she said. "And Parker, isn't it? I read your articles in *The Gazette*, of course. How can I help you?"

"We have a question for you and your husband."

"Great—let's find Eric. He's working on the plane."

The bright morning light ended just inside the hangar doors. Overhead, fluorescent tubes turned the shadowy interior to a murky gray. The Allington Tours single-propeller airplane stood in the middle of the concrete floor. Eric Gilder crouched under the fuselage, tinkering with the landing gear.

He must've heard our footsteps because he said, "Iris, sweetheart, any word on the plumbing? I hope we're not racking up a giant bill..."

"Eric," Iris said, escorting us to the plane. "We've got visitors."

Eric ducked out from under the fuselage. He wore his usual khaki-and-polo-shirt uniform. The same as Iris. He wiped his hands on a rag. Coming toward us, he smiled. The smile couldn't hide the fatigue in his face. Pale skin. Dark rings under his bloodshot eyes.

"Chief Lee, Parker," he said, acknowledging each of us with a nod. "What can I do for you?"

"We've got a photo we'd like to show you. It may help the investigation."

"Then I'm happy to help."

I held out my phone, and Eric and Iris gathered around.

The four of us in a huddle. I swiped through the photos of the car.

"Recognize it?" Mom asked.

Eric shrugged. "Hard to say. Lots of people drive Mercedes. Check half the garages on Chestnut Hill and you'll find a car like this one. And if it's not black, it's silver gray."

"What about you, Iris?"

Iris leaned closer. "Not sure. It's like Eric says—we know lots of people who drive a black Mercedes—and these photos are blurry."

"Can you name some of them?"

Iris backed away. She shook her head. "Not off the top of my head."

"Well, thanks for your help," Mom said. "We appreciate it."

We left them in the hangar. Outside in the morning sunshine, I pocketed my phone and said, "That was disappointing."

"Maybe. But if Iris knows people who own Mercedes, then why can't she give us some names?"

"Good point."

We moved past the office building on our left, with its big sign that said "Allington Tours." On our right, a lawn stretched down to docks on the lake. Four tour boats stood moored to the docks. In summer, they'd be taking tourists out around Gull Island and beyond.

The parking lot was a field of line stripes on the black-top. We passed the Tesla and Barry's van parked where it said, "Reserved for Staff." I climbed into Mom's cruiser. She fired up the engine, did a U-turn, and drove out of the lot.

As we drove, I sipped my coffee. I reflected on what we knew. It would be something if Mo's cameras revealed more details about the car. Maybe even the license plate. But what else did we have right now? Very little.

For some reason, I thought of the dent I'd seen at the inn. This was the kind of tiny detail that felt like it might mean something simply because the case was so muddled right now. But I mentioned it to Mom.

"Tell me exactly what you saw," she said, and pulled the cruiser to the shoulder of the road. She grabbed her cup of coffee and the remnants of her muffin and gave me her full attention. I felt a little silly describing my visit to room 9 at the Lakeview Inn, since the dent in the wall hardly seemed worthwhile mentioning.

"Your Aunt Lil expected me to wag my finger at you for going into that room, huh?"

"Yup. She loves to tease you."

"She sure does," Mom said with a chuckle. "Anyway, that dent may be nothing. Or it may be important. I expect to hear from forensics tomorrow. That might tell us if the dent is fresh or old—or if we need to revisit it."

Just then, a car whizzed past us on the road.

Mom raised an eyebrow. "Someone's asking for a speeding ticket."

"Mom," I said. "That was a Tesla."

"Eric and Iris. I bet they're heading home. And in a hurry. Maybe our questions about the photo jogged their memories..."

She turned on the engine again and pulled out onto the road, setting off after the Gilders' Tesla.

15

Outside the Gilder mansion stood Eric and Iris's Tesla. I got out of Mom's cruiser. But while she headed for the front door, I stopped by the garage. One of the doors was open. Inside, in the gloom stood a vintage red Aston Martin.

"Come on, Park," Mom said.

"Hold on."

I slipped into the garage. The three doors led to a single, large space. Next to the Aston Martin stood an SUV. Maybe that was Mrs. Gilder's more "practical" car. It blocked the view of the rest of the garage, and it wasn't until I'd rounded it that I saw the vehicle beyond it.

"Bingo."

I grinned at the black Mercedes as I snapped a photo. This time making sure I got a clear shot of the license plate number.

As I emerged from the darkness, I saw Mom was talking on her radio. Coming closer, I could hear Deputy Douglas's voice.

"—and you won't believe whose car it was Mo's camera caught?"

"Mrs. Gilder's," I said, loud enough for Mom and Deputy Douglas to hear.

"Oh," Deputy Douglas said. "Hi, Parker. Yeah, you're right. It's a match. The black Mercedes belongs to Mrs. Gilder."

I pointed a thumb over my shoulder at the garage. "It's back there, Mom."

"Good work," Mom said. "Both of you."

She ended the radio call with Deputy Douglas and gestured for me to follow her to the front door of the mansion. She rang the bell. A moment later, Dave the Butler opened.

"Mrs. Gilder is occupied," he said stiffly.

"We'll wait," Mom said.

"She has a packed schedule."

"She'll want to unpack it."

Mom stared him down. But if she was pushy, he was unmovable. A professional stick up his butt. It created an impasse.

Which Mom broke by leaning forward and whispering, "Dave, listen. You and I know about that DUI incident. And the pill problem you had. But Mrs. Gilder doesn't, does she? How about we keep it that way?"

Dave stared. No emotion. But something was going on inside that well-groomed head of his. Because he stepped aside.

"Be my guest," he muttered, a frown on his face.

I followed Mom inside. We stood in the mansion's massive entrance hall, which had more light pouring into it today. So I could actually see all the fancy stuff. Marble floors.

Oil portraits on the walls. Pedestals with vases and statuettes. Through arched doorways, I glimpsed antique furniture that would probably go for a fortune at a Sotheby's auction.

A wide staircase—wider than many homes in Allington—rose to a landing. Eric Gilder appeared at the top. He hurried down the stairs, one hand on the banister. Iris appeared behind him. Both still wearing their polo shirts and khakis.

"I'm afraid my mother is busy," he said.

"We'll wait," Mom said, crossing her arms on her chest. "All day if necessary."

"It would be better if you came back."

"Better for whom?"

Eric closed his mouth. Tight-lipped silence.

I joined Mom at her side and said, "You lied to us about the car. You did recognize it."

Eric frowned, still gripping the banister. Iris stepped down the staircase to stand at our level. She said, "Look, I'm sorry. We did recognize it. But we were being honest: so many people have a Mercedes. We didn't want to jump to any conclusions." She gestured at me. "Especially in front of a journalist."

"So you came back here to warn Mrs. Gilder."

"We came back here," Iris said, "to talk to her. Did we ask her about the car? Yes, we did."

"And what did she say?" Mom cut in.

Iris exchanged looks with her husband. He shrugged and said, "Mom can decide for herself what she wants to say. It's not like she can deny it was her car." He looked down at us again. "The truth is, we know no more than you do. I was shocked to recognize her car—and even more shocked when Mom admitted it was hers."

"Where is your mother?" Mom asked.

"Upstairs," Eric said. "On an important call."

"With whom?"

"How should I know?" He grimaced. "She wouldn't unlock the door to her room. She simply said she was in an important meeting. My mom's like the military. She operates on a need to know basis, and half the time I don't need to know."

"How do you feel about that?" I asked.

He looked at me, his lip curling. Distaste. "You think I'll dish out dirt on my family? And to a tabloid reporter?"

The Gazette might be a backwater paper. But it was no tabloid. Dad would often cut a story if he felt it was too mean spirited. In his view, the paper's role in town was to bring the truth to light while also nurturing a stronger sense of community. So calling *The Gazette* a tabloid was absurd and offensive.

"I think—" I began.

But Mom stopped me with a nudge. "Easy, Park. Easy."

She was right, of course. I shouldn't let Eric Gilder rile me up. And more importantly, I should cut him some slack. He was upset. After all, his brother had been murdered.

I took a deep breath. I breathed out, letting the anger go.

Iris was holding on to her husband's arm. She whispered in his ear. He frowned and said, "Well, I don't like journalists."

Iris turned back to us. "I'm sorry. My husband's touchy about this stuff."

"Touchy?" Eric snorted. "That's one word for it."

"Back when Ralph left," Iris explained, "there were stories in *The Gazette* about it. Stories that hinted at dark secrets and nasty in-fighting in the family. So forgive us for reacting strongly—we've been burned before."

"Was any of it true?" I asked. "The stories of in-fighting and the dark secrets?"

Iris smiled. Her eyes as hard as flint. But her voice was measured and polite when she said, "I'm doing my best to be helpful and civil. We could simply ask you to leave, you know."

"You could," Mom said, equally measured and polite. "And then I could haul you all down to the station for questioning."

"There's no need for that," a voice from above said.

Eric and Iris turned. Mrs. Gilder appeared at the top of the stairs, looking down at us. She wore the same clothes as before. Grays and blacks. Mourning.

Slowly, she descended the stairs. Taking her time. Aware that she was the center of attention. As confident as a queen.

"You have questions, I suppose," she said with a regal weariness. As if we were all oh-so tiring. "I may be able to answer some of them."

Halfway down the stairs, she stopped. Over her shoulder, she called out, "Nell, you can come down now. There's no point in hiding anymore."

A moment passed. Then a woman appeared on the landing at the top of the stairs. She paused. Hand resting on cocked hip. All attitude.

I drew in a sharp breath. Black baseball cap. Bomber jacket. That was her: the intruder.

16

"**A**bsolutely out of the question," Eric Gilder said, as he strode into the Gilder mansion library. "I want her out of here, and right away."

He was pointing at me.

"Calm down, sweetheart," Iris said, rubbing Eric's back. "I'm sure there's no harm in—"

"You've got to be kidding. No harm in a tabloid journalist sitting in on our private family conversation?"

"This is hardly a private conversation," Mom said. "In fact, this is very much on the record."

From her perch on the leather sofa, Mrs. Gilder glared at her son. "Sit down, Eric, and stop whining."

Eric frowned, but he hunched his shoulders like a contrite kid and he did as he was told: he sat down next to his mom. Iris hurried over to Mrs. Gilder's other side.

Mom remained standing, leaning against the massive hearth. I was already seated. The leather armchair under me creaked every time I breathed. Near me sat Nell, the burglar. Who, it turned out, was not a burglar.

"My name's Nell Shamus," she said. "I'm a private detective."

I raised an eyebrow. "Doesn't *shamus* mean detective?"

"I guess it does."

"So your name is 'Nell Detective, the detective'?"

I tried not to smile. I really did.

Nell gave me a stone-cold look. "My family name is Shamus. It's Irish."

"Go ahead, Miss Shamus," Mom said, giving me a disapproving frown.

The butler, Dave, moved around the room, handing out refreshments. He handed me a glass of sparkling water with a slice of lemon. He'd reverted to his professional behavior, though when he delivered the glass of mineral water to my mom, he asked her solicitously if she needed anything else. She waved him away.

"Mrs. Gilder is my client," Nell continued. "She's been kind enough to let me stay here while I'm in town."

"I saw you here at the house," I said. "Mrs. Gilder, you were signaling to Nell to get away from the window."

Nell grimaced. "A slip-up on my part."

"And you broke into the Lakeview Inn and The Allington Gazette's offices," Mom said. "Care to mention any other legal infractions?"

"It was trespassing at the inn," Nell said. "Though I'll admit I picked the piece-of-pie lock at *The Gazette.* I was hoping to find information on Ralph Gilder." She nodded at Mrs. Gilder. "For my client."

Mrs. Gilder gave an acknowledging nod.

Nell said, "I've been tracking Ralph Gilder for a year now. Mrs. Gilder employed a different detective before me. But I've had more luck. I found Ralph Gilder across the country. He moved from state to state, always under assumed names. He was a slippery guy."

"Hey," Eric said. "I don't appreciate you talking about my brother that way."

"Eric," Mrs. Gilder said. "Shut up and listen."

Eric frowned. But he shut his mouth.

Nell went on. "Ralph's racket was to look for loners who were dying. He'd insinuate himself. Become their best friends. Then he'd steal their identities for a few months, collecting their social security and selling off their possessions. Until someone caught on. A neighbor. A relative. Sometimes even the authorities. Then he'd skip town and start over someplace else."

"Charming," I said.

"You're being facetious," Nell said. "But actually, that's a good way to describe Ralph. He was charming. He could be incredibly likable. And, at the same time, down to earth. He always wore simple clothes. Nothing ostentatious. Jeans. T-shirts. A beige jacket. He was the guy next door. So bland and charming and trustworthy that he'd be the last person you'd suspect."

"Like at your local church," I said, and for a moment thought of Marina Kemp.

"Yes, even your local minister."

"No, he didn't."

Nell nodded. "For a while, Ralph pretended to be a Lutheran minister. Hoodwinked a lot of people. One woman said he knew Scripture so well—how could she *not* trust him? I spoke with people from a small-town congregation who were convinced he'd been an ordained minister staying with relatives nearby. He helped out at the church, quickly becoming part of the community. After he bled them dry, he skipped town. It's all in my report."

In room 9 at the Lakeview Inn, we'd found that Bible. Open to the story of the prodigal son. There was a line that came back to me—something about the son saying he wasn't worthy. That was what Ralph had told Ashley. So he'd prepared for his meeting with his ex-girlfriend by studying the Bible, looking for the language to manipulate her, the way he'd manipulated so many others. What a creep.

Nell continued: "Eventually, I tracked Ralph to Allington. From what I could tell, he was running out of money. That's why he came home."

Eric turned to his mom. "And knowing all this, you still wanted to bring Ralph back home? After what he'd done to us? What he was still doing to so many others?"

Iris leaned forward so she could talk to Eric over her mom's lap. "Eric, sweetheart, now's not the time..." she cooed at him.

Mrs. Gilder ignored them. "Nell asked me what to do now that Ralph was back in town, and I assured her it was our opportunity to reel him in. But we needed to discover what his plans were, of course. I gave my chauffeur the week off, so I could serve as Nell's driver. David is a fine chauffeur, but he can't keep his mouth shut, and I didn't want him blabbing all over town."

Dave stiffened at the mention of his name. But he didn't show any signs of otherwise wanting to defend his reputation.

Mom said, "And then we found your son on Gull Island."

Mrs. Gilder nodded. "I'd reached him too late. Nell and I carried on. I needed to know what happened to him. You involved your daughter in the investigation, completely against professional procedure. But I saw how it might be to my benefit. The police department is difficult to break into. But *The Gazette* was not."

Mom tsk-tsked. "You should've leveled with me instead."

"Ha," Mrs. Gilder barked. "I don't trust cops to do much, but eat donuts. Having said that—" She sighed. She stuck her chin out, and sounded more regal than ever when she said, "—I recognize that despite my wealth, you have resources I don't. Snitches. Forensics. Even that whiny deputy of yours must be good for something. Which is why I am calling Nell off and instead entirely trusting the Allington PD to solve my son's murder."

Nell shrugged. "Thanks, Mrs. G. I'll send you my invoice."

"How gracious of you to trust us, Mrs. Gilder," Mom said. "Especially since you've broken the law."

"Chief Lee." Mrs. Gilder straightened up. She raised a commanding finger. Her eyebrows clenched in a glare. "If you so much as hint at charging Nell Shamus or myself—or if I find you dawdling on this case, which ought to be your number one priority—I'll have my lawyers hounding you for the rest of your career. Which I can assure you will be short."

"Our number one priority is to find your son's killer," Mom assured her.

Mrs. Gilder, after her saber-rattling, seemed to deflate. She sank back into the sofa and folded her hands over her lap.

"Ralph did bad things, but he was still my son. He was so lost—and I hoped he could be found. Now he's dead and I'll never bring him back home. Truly bring him back home..."

She stared into space.

Eric reached around her, putting an arm over her shoulders.

"Oh, Mom," he said. "I'm sorry…"

His touch reignited her. She jerked away from him, shrugging his arm off. Eyes blazing, she glared at him.

"Stop it," she snapped. "Don't be disingenuous. You're not a hugger. And nor am I." She straightened up. Chin up. Stiff upper lip. "I didn't make it this far by sniveling. Nor did you."

An awkward silence fell on the gathering.

17

The encounter with Nell Shamus gave me and Mom lots to think about. And talk about at dinner. Usually, the whole family gathered for dinner on Sundays at Broadstairs House. Otherwise, it was just Mom, Dad, Scottie, Joy, and me, and we'd sit at the kitchen table. But tonight, Ray and Amy joined us, so Mom and I set the table in the dining room, laying out napkins, silverware, and colorful bowls my parents had brought back from a vacation to Guatemala.

Our big, geriatric Victorian house was bursting with activity. The house was full of voices—talking, laughter—which vied with the music Dad had put on the vintage stereo: the sprightly shuffle of Cuban jazz.

In the kitchen, Dad and Joy were tending to a giant pot of vegetarian chili. Amy was mashing up avocados for guacamole while Joy chopped tomatoes and onions and chili peppers for a homemade pico de gallo. Ray took responsibility for beer and tortilla chips. Scottie had a friend who imported hot sauces from Mexico, so his contribution was three kinds of salsa picante—a chili verde, a habanero, and a chipotle—and lots of commentary on the global market for salsas. More than anyone ever needed to know.

While Dad put the finishing touches on the chili, and Joy grated cheddar cheese, the rest of us hung out in the kitchen with them.

Dad was asking Joy about her yoga session tomorrow at Shepherd's Gate Church. Which was fully booked. Scottie was telling Ray about an idea he had for a new business—a cat cafe, where people would pay by the half hour for the opportunity to pet a cat. Mom questioned how Scottie would handle people with cat allergies. Or the fact that he'd admitted once to not liking cats. Ray cut in and said he understood: he himself preferred dogs, and then he launched into a story about Wimsey, his and Roxie's rambunctious Dalmatian.

"Don't tell Amy," I said. "Bunter might get upset."

Bunter was Amy's cat. But Amy didn't notice my little defense of her companion (and all other felines). She was standing in a corner between the wall and the pantry, holding an uneaten tortilla chip and staring into space. I left the others and joined her.

"You gonna eat that?" I asked, leaning against the wall next to her. "Or are you contemplating the theology of tortilla chips?"

She let out a long sigh.

"Oh," I said. "The fundraiser. How were sales and donations from last night's movie night?"

She nodded. "We did all right."

"That's great."

"But only *all right*. Once we take out the expenses associated with hosting the event, the proceeds are modest."

Scottie overheard us. "That's impossible. I sold out of snacks and drinks. Everything from Cafe Larke and the

Breeze was gone by the end of the night. In fact, halfway through I had to call to Joy to get her to run some extra brownies and coffee over from Cafe Larke. People couldn't get enough."

"And we probably would've made a loss if you hadn't sold so well," Amy said.

"Next time," Scottie said, "you should go big. Set up a full-sized concert stage and book musical acts. Well-known ones. How about this: the Allington Pop Festival. I've got the idea all mapped out. If you want to take a look..."

He dug out his smartphone and opened his note-taking app, ready to share his business plan. But Amy and I weren't paying attention. I took her free hand, the one not holding a tortilla chip, and squeezed it. "Maybe there's a mistake. Maybe you need to run the numbers again."

Amy shook her head. "Marina ran the numbers again. The result was the same."

I frowned, thinking of what I knew about Marina. Still, Amy had defended her, so I'd better tread carefully.

"But lots of people donated money—I saw them do it."

"Lots of small amount, I suppose."

I remembered the $50 bills I'd seen people hand over to Marina.

"Amy, what if Marina made a mistake?"

"Marina's always been reliable. She's a stickler for detail. In fact, she's always been so organized that I hardly have to get involved. Throughout the year, even during tax season, she runs our finances so smoothly, I never have to worry."

"Could she have any reason to make a mistake..." I paused. "...on purpose?"

Amy pulled her hand free from mine.

"What are you saying?"

"I'm just—" I paused. Hesitating because of the look of

horror on Amy's face. Then went on: "Look, it sounds like she's got full control of your finances. And it sounds like your fundraiser should've yielded more by now. Maybe something isn't right. Maybe—"

"Forget it, Park. Marina's devoted so much of her time and energy to volunteering for the church. For decades. She's the last person who'd want to hurt our community. The last person."

Dad joined us. "Amy's right, Park. I appreciate your suspicious mind. In fact, I pay you for it at *The Gazette*. But this is a case where we're dealing with a person who is above suspicion. I mean, Marina's practically a saint."

I held up my hands, surrendering to their united front.

"All right, all right, I believe you." I took Amy's hand again, trying to calm her. "Maybe there's some other thing we can do to help your church."

Amy sighed again. "I'm not sure what that would be."

"Family meeting," Dad hollered in answer.

"Family meeting," Mom echoed.

"And dinner's served!" he added.

Dad carried the pot of chili into the dining room. Joy followed with the bowl of cheddar cheese and then the rest of us came after with the various dishes and condiments. We sat down. Amy said grace. And then, once the food was being passed around, Dad said, "Family meeting in session. Let's help Amy figure out how she can raise more money for the church. Scottie—you're our idea man. You start."

The dining room came alive with sound. The clinking of glasses, rattling of knives and forks and spoons, scraping of bowls. Ray opened bottled beer and sodas, each making a satisfying pop and fizz. Meanwhile, everyone talked about how to help Amy.

I smiled as I listened.

This was how my family solved problems—together.

But even as they talked, a thought niggled at the back of my mind.

The thought that Amy ought to take a closer look at those numbers. The thought that maybe Marina wasn't entirely honest. Not a perfect saint.

18

The next day, I felt even more determined to discover more about Marina Kemp. The fundraising finances remained a mystery, and I was going to expose the truth. But as I was scrolling through *The Gazette*'s online records to find any references to Marina, Dad passed by my desk and saw what I was doing.

"Parker Lee, didn't I tell you to drop that?"

I shrugged. "It can't hurt to look."

"We've got lots of stories to focus on. This is not one of them. Amy's financial troubles are serious. But looking for a scapegoat is a risky thing. You could hurt Marina's reputation."

"Her snow white reputation," I said, unable to hide my skepticism.

He sighed. "Don't believe me? Why don't you talk to Balthazar? Marina used to do his bookkeeping. He might be able to clear things up for you. Now—" He circled our desks and sat down in his chair. He folded his interlaced fingers over his belly. "—tell me more about your meeting yesterday with the Gilders."

At the family dinner, Mom and I had provided a few highlights, but in the end, we'd spent most of the evening brainstorming ideas for Amy's fundraiser. So I straightened up in my chair and told Dad about our meeting with the Gilders. The revelation that the "burglar" was a detective hired by Mrs. Gilder. The tension in the room between Eric and his mother.

Dad chuckled. "That's classic Mrs. Gilder. She's as tough as nails."

"I can't make sense of them."

"The Gilders? Oh, it's like this: Mrs. Gilder is first-generation rich. Self-made. In fact, she's convinced she invented rags-to-riches. And she's likely to work hard until the day she dies."

"At which point Eric gets it all?"

"Well, yes—now that Ralph is gone."

I nodded. That made sense. And it suggested Eric had a motive to kill his brother. Assuming Mrs. Gilder hadn't cut the prodigal son out of her will.

Footsteps echoed through the old firehouse. I spun my chair around. Mom was striding down the aisle between empty desks, her uniform as pristine as always.

"We got it," she said, holding up a ream of papers. "We got the forensics report."

Dad got to his feet. He perched on the edge of my desk. I got up, too. We huddled around Mom. She pushed aside my keyboard and fanned out the pages. Like she was showing us her card hand. I hoped we'd been dealt a royal flush this time.

"As you know, Ralph Gilder only had a few possessions," she began. "One pair of jeans, khaki pants, a pair of white sneakers, a pair of brown loafers, five t-shirts, two white button-downs, a beige jacket, and, of course, a red scarf. The tests on his duffel bag and the clean clothes revealed nothing out of interest."

"And the clothes he was found in?"

"That's a different story."

Mom quirked a smile. This was about as excited as she ever got. She'd found something big. I could feel it.

"What?"

"Dirt from where he lay on the island. But also synthetic fibers."

"All right," I said, my heart sinking. Synthetic fibers hardly sounded big. "Which tells us what?"

"They match the carpeting in his room."

"So he lay on the floor. Big deal. Maybe he lay down to do yoga. Or to grab something he'd dropped."

Then I thought of the dent I'd found in the wall. My heart beat faster. An idea was taking shape in my mind, but I couldn't quite put words to it yet.

"He lay on the floor and kicked the wall..."

Mom nodded. "Ralph Gilder's body had signs of *livor mortis* on his back, indicating that he died on his back and lay for a while face upward. But we found him face-down on the island, remember? The forensic team examined the hotel room. They found traces of human skin in the carpeting's fabric. Fabric that they found adhering to the corpse. Which suggests not only prolonged contact but also rubbing—signs of a struggle."

"Wait a minute." I gaped at her. "You're saying that—"

Mom broke into a full smile. "Yes, I am. Ralph didn't die on Gull Island. The killer strangled him in his hotel room and then moved him. We're rethinking the crime scene. I'm meeting the county coroner and the state police at the Lakeview Inn in 20 minutes."

I got to my feet. "Let's go."

But Mom put a hand on my shoulder and shook her head, a sad look on her face.

19

I strode down Main Street, fists dug into my pockets. I couldn't believe Mom was actively cutting me out of the investigation. Because of the county coroner and the state police. They didn't feel the same way Mom did about family involvement in murder cases. Or any other cases, for that matter.

Of course, rationally, I understood. But it still felt like a betrayal, when Mom usually included me in her work.

I headed toward Cafe Larke, feeling the need for a double espresso. And maybe one of Joy's double-fudge brownies. Or a whole tray.

I came to a standstill at the corner of Peony and Main. Racks of books stood on the sidewalk with rows and rows of used hard- and paperbacks.

Balthazar Books. Of course. I nearly forgot.

I pulled my hands out of my pockets.

Well, if Mom wouldn't let me investigate Ralph Gilder's murder, then Dad wasn't going to stop me from looking into Marina Kemp.

I stepped into the independent store.

Shelves lined the walls, reaching from the floor to the ornate tin ceiling. Tables crowded the tiled floor. At Balthazar Books, I was always inching past people or bumping into edges and knocking books down. The tagline ought to be "Chock-full of books."

Balthazar stood behind the counter at the back, ringing up a purchase for a customer. While I waited for him to be done, I browsed the section of mystery novels. A new Sara Paretsky. Hardback. I fingered the pages, wishing I could justify paying so much for a book. I slipped it back into place, promising myself that as soon as it came out in paperback I'd buy it. Instead, I looked at a paperback mystery by Ellery Adams I hadn't read yet.

As I was reading the blurb on the back, I sensed someone standing near me. I glanced over and saw a tall man with a shaved head. He was wearing brown robes. As he read the spines of the books on the shelf, he cocked his head. He was in the Religion/Spirituality section. And obviously a Buddhist monk.

A group of Buddhists had founded a monastery many years ago, building a cluster of cabins in the Allington Woods. They organized meditation retreats. It had started small. But it grew and grew as word spread. Today, the White Pine Monastery consisted of several buildings and beautiful grounds set in a forest glade.

Occasionally, the Buddhists or visiting practitioners appeared in town. But I often didn't see them for weeks or months, especially during the winter, when the monastery hosted only a few events.

As I was considering this, Balthazar approached me. A small, thin man with wire-rim glasses and a black goatee. Button-down shirt with a cardigan over it. He looked like a cozy incarnation of Mephistopheles. His smile, as always, was kind and welcoming.

"So, Parker," he said. "What book are you wanting today?"

"No book, Balthazar. I'm looking for information. About Marina Kemp."

"A name I know well. What about her?"

"She used to do your accounting."

"You journalists know all our dirty secrets."

"Dirty secrets?"

Balthazar waved away the insinuation. "I was being clever. In reality, there's nothing to tell. She used to do my bookkeeping, that's all."

"Used to. You let her go?"

"No, no. She stopped. She retired—oh, it must be 4 years ago now. So I found someone else."

"Did you ever have any trouble with her?"

"Trouble?" He raised one of his arched eyebrows. "What kind of trouble?"

I shrugged. "Like inaccuracies. Money disappearing."

Balthazar frowned. "Parker, are you asking me if Marina ever skimmed the books?"

I bit my lip. When he put it like that, it made me feel awful. But I had to sort this out. For Amy's sake.

"Yes, I guess I am asking that..."

Balthazar shook his head emphatically. "No. Never. Marina was the kind of accountant everyone raves about: a steady, reliable professional. She never tried to play fast and loose with the numbers. She was the tortoise, not the hare." He scratched his beard, thinking. "If I remember correctly, she didn't much want to retire, either. It wasn't about the money. She loved her work. But with her mom getting sick, she had to cut down on hours, and if she retired, she could activate her pension. Which wasn't much, but with her mom so sick, she had no choice. So she shut her business and doubled down on volunteering instead."

"That's right," a voice said near us. It was the Buddhist monk. He smiled. "Apologies for butting in on your conversation, but I couldn't help but overhear you talking about Marina."

I introduced myself as Parker Lee, journalist with *The Allington Gazette*. His name was Brother Danan, and he told me he knew both my sisters well: Joy because of her involvement in meditation retreats and Amy because the two communities supported each other.

"That's great," I said. "It's actually Shepherd's Gate Church and its fundraiser that I'm doing a story on. But you say you know Marina?"

"That's right," he said. "Marina volunteered to do our accounting at the monastery."

"But she stopped?"

"We were grateful for her generosity. But we no longer needed her services."

"Oh?"

He smiled. "Nothing like that. We didn't dismiss her because of any wrongdoing. She was wonderful. Conscientious. Meticulous. Always making suggestions that benefitted us, like setting up a fund to manage our money."

"You mean navigating the IRS?"

He laughed. "You certainly are quick to suspect."

Heat rose to my face. "I didn't mean to—"

He raised a hand, palm outward. "Don't worry. I'm teasing. We monks enjoy teasing." He winked. Then grew serious. "But I want to make clear that Marina never did anything unethical. We're not interested in dodging taxes. I'm talking about spreading out funds, so if we made a lot of money during our summer retreat, we could put the excess into our fund for the leaner months. We want everything to run smoothly, and Marina was exceptionally good at that. For a volunteer, we could never have hoped for better."

"And yet you let her go."

"It was the responsible thing to do. We were growing rapidly, and Marina had other clients and responsibilities, including Shepherd's Gate Church. She's remarkably committed to faith communities and nonprofits in Allington. But at White Pine Monastery, accounting had become a full-time job. Also, quite frankly, we preferred to have a business administrator who lived with us. Today, one of our own monks handles the financials."

"I see."

He smiled again. "I'm glad you do."

Balthazar adjusted his glasses as he looked up at the tall Brother Danan.

"Did you find what you were looking for?"

"I did." Brother Danan held up a book on Kierkegaard, the 19th century Danish theologian and philosopher. "A little light bedtime reading."

Balthazar chuckled. Then turned to me. "And what about you, Parker—did you find what you were looking for?"

I sighed. "Yeah, thank you both."

But the truth was that I was disappointed. A portrait of Marina was emerging: steadfast, detail-oriented, ethical. Above suspicion. Exactly what Amy and Dad kept telling me. All the facts suggested they were right.

But my gut still told me something was wrong. And if half of Allington insisted Marina was a saint, there was only one person left I could talk to about her track record.

Marina herself.

20

Anarrow driveway—empty now—led to the small ranch-style house. Aluminum siding. A lawn so small you could park it in the Gilders' garage. But it was more homely than the Chestnut Hill mansion. Flower boxes under the windows on either side of the front door overflowed with yellow and red nasturtiums. On the door, a handmade sign said, "Welcome to our home."

I rang the doorbell.

When no one came to the door, I knocked.

I stepped back and peered through a window. Gauzy curtains obscured the interior, turning the furniture into shadowy shapes.

No one home.

I looked around. I should've guessed Marina wasn't home since the driveway was empty.

Over at the neighbor's, only a few paces away, a middle-aged man was mowing his lawn with an old-school push mower. He wore a baseball cap, jeans, and a t-shirt with a cartoon tortoise that said, "Life in the Fast Lane."

As I approached, he stopped and took off his baseball cap. Ran a hand over his brow, wiping off the sweat.

"It's hard work pushing this thing. But luckily my little lawn doesn't require a lot." He smiled. "You looking for Marina?"

I nodded. "Any idea when she'll be back?"

"You rang the bell and knocked? Did you knock real hard?"

"Pretty hard—why?"

"Ophelia's hard of hearing, and not so mobile these days. But I bet she's out, too." He shook his head, his smile gone. "Which ain't a good sign."

I remembered something Balthazar said about Marina's mom being sick.

"You think Marina took her mom somewhere?"

"Not just anywhere. They'll be at the doc's, for sure. That Ophelia's been sick for a long time, and by now, I reckon they know the doctor's office about as well as they know their own home."

"I'm sorry to hear that," I said, and discovered that I really was sorry. "Are they close? Marina and her mom?"

"I should say so. Marina never married, and Ophelia's hubby—Marina's daddy—he died many years ago. Marina is Ophelia's only kid. If you can call a grown woman a kid." He chuckled. "My own daddy is ninety-three years old, and I'm still his little boy. But he's got his buddies at the retirement home, and I've got my wife and kids." He gestured toward Marina and Ophelia's home. "They've only got each other. And pretty soon Marina will be alone."

I thanked him and headed back to my car.

A heavy weight pressed down on my heart. Even though I knew it would one day happen, I couldn't imagine losing my mom and dad. But I knew that when the time came, Amy, Joy, Ray, Scottie, and I would support each other.

Marina had no one.

The weight on my chest pushed harder and harder, and tears surprised me by filling my eyes. What had gotten into me? I was here to investigate whether Marina was stealing money from Amy.

I couldn't let my sympathy for Marina distract me. Yes, it was sad that her mom was sick. But if she really was stealing, I had a responsibility to expose the truth.

I wiped the tears away.

21

That evening, I stepped into Shepherd's Gate Church, and I looked around for Marina. Something clenched in my chest. Worry. But worry about what? Obviously, I told myself, it's worry about Amy, and whether Marina's stealing.

Joy was laying out yoga mats on the raised platform by the altar, so they'd circle her own in the middle. Amy came hurrying down the aisle toward me.

"Thank God you're here, Park."

"Yes, here I am," I said, distracted, still looking around to spot Marina.

Amy slipped an arm around mine and turned me around. Together, we moved back the way I'd come.

"Where are we going?" I asked.

"To the front of house. I need you to handle tickets and donations."

I was taken aback. "But how will Marina feel about that?"

"She's not coming tonight, after all. Didn't you hear?"

Amy stopped us. She gave my arm a squeeze, as if preparing me for bad news. "Marina's mom was hospitalized, and I think her time might be coming."

I nodded. "I heard she wasn't well."

"After Joy's yoga and then meditation, I'm going to lead everyone in prayer. For Ophelia, so that she doesn't suffer more than necessary as she passes from this life. And for Marina, to support her in her grief." She looked thoughtful. "In the days ahead, I'll devote some time to thinking about how we can best support Marina. She'll be losing her life-long companion, her mother, but we'll make sure she's not alone."

As Amy began to detail the things the congregation could do—bring lasagna, drop in for daily check-ins, and just sit silently with her in her grief—the weight on my heart grew heavier, and I could feel the tears threatening me again.

I tried to conjure my old suspicions about Marina again. But I couldn't. Even as I reminded myself that my concerns about theft were valid, I couldn't stomach my old feelings— they seemed crass and inappropriate.

Maybe I'd been wrong about Marina. Everyone else seemed to think I was wrong, after all, and it didn't seem fair to level my suspicion at someone who was experiencing such pain.

I sat at the table by the entrance. The cash and the donation boxes stood on the table next to a clipboard with a printout of people who'd reserved a spot for tonight's event. The list was long.

Amy brought me a bottle of water. "Do you want coffee, too?"

I shook my head, and remembering how I'd plied

Marina with coffee to get her away from the donation box, felt heat rise to my face.

I'd treated her unfairly. I'd convinced myself I was right—that I knew better than everyone else—and if I'd had the chance to "expose" Marina, I could've caused serious damage.

I took a deep breath. If I wanted to do some good, I should focus on helping Marina instead. Like Amy was planning to help her.

"Let's open up," Amy said. "Here."

She handed me the keys to the cash and the donation boxes.

Then she unlocked the double doors to the church and swung them outward, securing them with their hook latches. People filed inside, and soon I was busy checking guests off the list, handling money for the tickets, and stuffing cash into the donation box.

I expected the ticket sales to keep me busy, with the occasional donation adding to my work. But the donations were frequent.

First, a woman handed me two $20 bills. A man gave me two $50 bills. Then an elderly woman who looked like she was fit enough to run a marathon leaned over the table and whispered, "I made my big donation at the movie night—$500—which I hope will do some good."

"I'm—" I was flummoxed. "I'm sure it will."

A man behind her, apparently overhearing her, held out a wad of cash. "Hear, hear. I love this place."

I took the money and asked if he needed a receipt for tax deductible purposes.

"Nah," he said. "I usually just stuff bills straight into the donation box without any fanfare. Feel free to do the same."

He moved down the aisle toward Joy and the yoga mats,

not waiting around to see me do just that: stuff his donation into the box. And after his donation, more poured in.

People in Allington were so incredibly generous.

Amy joined me. "How're we doing?"

"Incredibly well. All those ideas we brainstormed at dinner the other night must be paying off."

Amy gave me a confused look. "What do you mean? Those ideas are for the next fundraiser."

"You mean, you didn't do anything to try to get more donations or tickets sales?"

Amy shook her head. "This event was already sold out last week. And it looks like we've got just as many people as we did when we hosted the movie night on Tuesday. Or at the other events, for that matter."

"Huh," I said.

So this night wasn't so different from Tuesday—or the other events. Which suggested the total amount of donations might be more or less the same.

Amy joined Joy by the altar. The event was about to begin.

After the last person had paid for their ticket and handed me a $40 contribution, I closed the front doors. Back at the table, I stuck the little key into the lock on the donation box and pried the top open.

Inside, the cash nearly reached the top.

My heart sank. I didn't need to count all the bills in the box to know that the amount far, far exceeded what the church had raised on Tuesday. Even if, for some reason, tonight's guests donated more, it could never explain the big discrepancy.

There was only one explanation, and I wished it weren't true.

The donation box had been full on Tuesday, too. But a large part of it had vanished. Marina had taken it.

22

The next afternoon, I left *The Gazette* and joined Aunt Lil in the Lakeview Inn's reception. The state police, county coroner, and Mom had vacated the premises and, Dad had told me, were meeting at the Allington PD to discuss the case. Apparently, Mom was looking closer at Mrs. Gilder and whether her choice to hire Nell Shamus wasn't just about getting information. Nell Shamus had a checkered past. Could Mrs. Gilder have hired her to find Ralph and kill him? It sounded far-fetched to me, but Dad insisted that the state police and county corner supported that theory.

Since I was still excluded, I decided I could make myself useful by helping Aunt Lil clean up the inn.

"I'm glad you could help clean," Aunt Lil said, handing me a mop, and then frowned. "But frankly, you ought to clean up your aura first. It's a mess."

I shrugged. "Guess it's the investigation."

I didn't want to tell her about my restless night and the endless thoughts about Marina. Should I tell Amy what I'd discovered and expose Marina? Or should I keep quiet? Either option felt like a failure.

"Are we cleaning up room 9?" I asked.

Just then, Zadie came down the stairs. She said, "All done. The basement will be the big job."

Aunt Lil nodded. "Come on. I'll show you."

We headed down the stairs to the basement, carrying buckets, mops, and brooms. At the bottom, we stopped, the three of us surveying the damage. The leak had wreaked havoc. Water-logged magazines lay scattered across the floor. An old sofa had gained a dark skirt of dirt or mold, and Aunt Lil decreed that it would have to go. Several antique wooden chairs were salvageable, but they would need a thorough scrub. The concrete floor itself was filthy.

We got started by tidying up, gathering all the detritus— the ruined magazines—and stacking them near the basement stairs, so we could carry it out to the trash. Then Zadie and I carried the sofa upstairs. A heavy lift. We left it on the porch—we'd have to take it to the town dump. Back in the basement, we scrubbed the chairs and stacked them. Then began mopping the floor.

As we mopped, I noticed how close the water had come to the shelves that lined the walls. Here, Aunt Lil kept all kinds of antiques and extra blankets and other items, many fairly valuable.

"Lucky the basement didn't flood more than it did," I said.

Aunt Lil nodded. "And lucky Barry had time to come urgently."

"Of course," I said. "I almost forgot that Barry was here, fixing the plumbing. Wait a minute." I stopped mopping. "Aunt Lil, you discovered the flooded basement early Thursday morning, right? And when did Barry arrive?"

"Oh, almost right away."

"And did he stay the whole day?"

"No, he was in and out. He stopped the leak and then he left to get supplies. I got busy with other things, but I do remember seeing his van outside around lunchtime."

"And did you see him later that day—in the afternoon or evening?"

Aunt Lil shook her head. "It doesn't mean he wasn't here, though. We already talked to your mom about this. Zadie didn't see him, either—did you, Zadie?"

Zadie nodded. She kept her eyes on her mopping and didn't stop. Something about her reluctance to look up made me suspicious.

"Zadie?" I asked. "Did you see Barry in the afternoon?"

"No, like I told your mom, I didn't see him."

A firm no. A clear statement. But still, Zadie didn't look up.

Intuition tingled in my fingertips. I moved over to Zadie and blocked her way. I put a hand on her mop, forcing her to stop.

"Zadie, you didn't *see* Barry. But do you know whether he was at the inn that afternoon?"

She glanced up, and her eyes had the harried look of an animal that was trapped and scared.

"Barry's a good guy," she said. "I don't want to say anything that I can't prove. It might get him into trouble."

She tried to pull the mop out of my hands, so she could keep working, but I held on.

"What happened, Zadie? What haven't you told us?"

"Zadie," Aunt Lil said. "We won't be mad. And, of course, we won't jump to any conclusions about Barry. Will we, Park?"

I shook my head. "Of course not."

Zadie let out a sigh. She loosened her hold on the mop, letting me take it. She wrapped her hands around her midriff, hugging herself. "All right. It's true that I didn't see Barry. But in the afternoon, I had to make up a room on the second floor. I was bringing up fresh sheets and towels when I noticed something. Footprints in the hallway."

"Footprints?" I said. "Like muddy prints?"

Zadie shook her head. "Wet prints. Someone had walked down the corridor and back again in very wet boots. Barry wore heavy work boots, and when I saw him come out of the basement once, he left wet prints in the reception area. By the time I came out of room 15, which I was preparing, the wet marks had disappeared, absorbed by the carpeting. But..."

"But what?"

"I noticed that the boot prints stopped in front of a door."

Zadie bit her lip.

I said, "It was the door to room 9, wasn't it?"

Zadie nodded.

23

Ashley, over by the counter, was pulling on a jacket when Mom and I stepped into Cafe Larke. She swung a purse around her shoulder and waved to Joy.

"See you tomorrow."

"Heading home for the day?" Mom asked, holding open the door for her.

Ashley nodded. "I'm walking over to Ariel's pre-school."

"We'll walk with you."

Turning onto Main Street, we walked side-by-side, Mom and I flanking Ashley. She talked about her schedule. About Ariel's pre-school. About the weather. Occasionally, she reached for a loose strand of hair and tugged at it. A nervous gesture.

"You know why we'd like to talk to you?" Mom asked.

"It's about Ralph."

"Did you know Ralph asked your dad for money?"

Ashley closed her eyes, briefly, and then looked at Mom again. "I guessed he would."

"And did you know your dad got the money out to pay Ralph?"

"Oh, Dad…" she said with a sigh.

We'd arrived at the pre-school and Ashley reached for the door, but Mom grabbed the handle, as if to open for her. Instead, she held the door shut.

"Ashley, where was your dad on Thursday afternoon? That was the day Ralph died."

"He was working. He already told you. He was driving around, from client to client. He was nowhere near Gull Island."

"Did he go to the Lakeview Inn?"

Ashley looked thoughtful. Then nodded. "I think so. When he came home for dinner, his overalls were wet, especially at the bottom. He stuffed wads of newspaper into his boots. I guess they were wet. He said the Lakeview had a bad leak in the basement."

Mom looked at me. I gave her a nod.

"Where is Barry now?" I asked.

"Working, of course."

"We tried to call him, but he didn't answer."

"He rarely does. He's terrible with technology. But he should be home soon." Ashley frowned. "What's all this about? Why are you asking so many questions about my dad?" Then her eyes widened. She shook her head, emphatically. "No. My dad would never—he didn't hurt Ralph. My dad's one of the good guys."

Mom nodded. She pulled open the door. "Go ahead, Ashley. Go find Ariel. Then we'll all go home to see your dad."

We watched Ashley disappear inside, and I thought of what she'd said—*my dad's one of the good guys*—and I couldn't help but think of Marina. Everyone thought of her as one of the good guys, too. But how much did we really know about our neighbors?

No one was infallible. Sometimes even the good guys, put under massive pressure, could miss the mark and do something bad.

24

Since Ashley didn't own a car, she, her daughter, and I walked across town to the Waterstons' home. Mom, picking up her cruiser, met us out front. She'd parked on the street. Barry's van stood parked in the driveway, leaving no space for other vehicles.

Ariel tugged at her mom's hand. "Let's go see Grampa!"

"I knocked," she said. "No answer."

Ashley looked surprised, taking a step onto the lawn. "Really? He should be home."

An odd feeling crawled across my back, making the hairs on my neck stand up. I put out a hand, telling Ashley and Ariel to stay back. I glanced over at Mom.

"Maybe we should check out the house first," I said.

"I agree," Mom said.

She tried the front door. It was locked. But Ashley dug into her purse and brought out her bundle of keys, and a moment later, Mom and I were stepping into the house.

Behind us, Ariel cried out, "Momma, why can't we go in? I wanna go in!"

We walked down the hallway. A doorway to the left revealed a small living room. Through a doorway to the right, a bedroom. Everything was quiet. Down the corridor, the kitchen came into view. The table. The counter. The back door, standing slightly ajar.

The creepy-crawly sensation slid down between my shoulder blade. Goosebumps broke out across my arms.

"Mom," I whispered. "I've got a bad feeling…"

"Me too…"

She put a hand on her holster, ready to draw her gun.

In the kitchen, we found Barry sitting at the table. My first thought was that he was exhausted from a long day at work and had laid his head down on the table to rest.

Mom's sharp intake of breath warned me I was wrong.

She leaped forward and put a hand to Barry's neck.

"Weak pulse," she said, and then tapped the two-way radio strapped to her chest. "Deputy, 10-52. Need an ambulance urgently at the Waterstons' home." She rattled off the address.

Meanwhile, I took a closer look at Barry. He was lying on the table, face turned to the side, arms crooked around his head. Next to him on the tabletop sat a plate with the remnants of a handful of potato chips and a long kosher pickle. A half-empty glass of ginger ale. The fizzy bubbles still swimming in the copper liquid. A white powder smudged the lip of the glass.

And next to that: a pill jar and a scattering of capsules—each one opened and emptied.

"Oh, no," I said. I moved around the table. Something stuck out from under Barry, pinned there by his right arm.

A piece of paper.

Mom had seen it too, and fitting a latex glove on her

hand, she slid it out from under Barry's arm. I cocked my head to read it. Typewritten words. Two simple sentences that took my breath away.

I'M SORRY. I DID WHAT I THOUGHT WAS BEST.

25

In the waiting room at Holloway Hospital, the clock on the wall made its relentless circuit as Ashley, Ariel, and I waited for news about Barry. A TV on the wall played endless nature shows, aerial shots of Scotland and Hawaii and the Sahara desert. As if to remind us the world was still a beautiful place. Or simply to distract us.

Outside the long bank of windows, night had fallen. Deep, dark night. It felt as if dawn might never come again.

Ariel colored in a coloring book. Then wanted to play with the blocks and other toys at a small table for kids.

"I'm going to build a house," she said.

Ashley, tears trickling silently down her face, nodded. She'd been crying on and off for hours.

Ariel put a hand on her mom's back and rubbed it. She said, with surprising adult compassion, "Mommy, it's going to be all right. You'll see."

Ashley pulled her daughter to her, hugging her hard.

"Mommy," Ariel said. "Too tight. You're crushing me."

But then she leaned into her mom's hug. Even this five-year-old knew how to comfort. And yet I felt at a loss. What could I do for Ashley? Nothing. I felt powerless. And somehow responsible, too, as if I'd caused Barry to attempt suicide. But I didn't make him do it. I couldn't even imagine Barry himself doing it.

Amy would know what to do in a situation like this. But Amy wasn't here. So Parker Lee would have to do.

After Ariel left to play at the little table, I took the seat next to Ashley.

"Can I get you something to drink or eat?" I asked.

Ashley shrugged. "I'm not hungry."

"I'll get you a coffee and a bottle of water. If you don't want it, you can just leave it."

Halfway out of my seat, I stopped. The doctor was turning into the waiting room, an unreadable expression on her face.

Ashley saw what I saw and shot to her feet.

"My dad—" Her voice dropped to a whisper. "—is he gone?"

A clatter of blocks. A small chair overturning. And then Ariel slipped under her mom's arm, wrapping herself around her. Her courage—*it's going to be all right, you'll see*—replaced with a tremble and eyes glistening with tears.

"Your dad's in stable condition," the doctor said. She crouched down to speak to Ariel. "Your granddad's doing all right."

Ariel buried her face in Ashley's side.

Ashley was gripping her daughter tight.

"Will he—will he live?" she asked.

The doctor straightened up. "Yes, he'll pull through. He'll still be unconscious for a few more hours, at least. Maybe longer. Given the dose he ingested, I'd say he's got weeks of recovery ahead of him. He got here just in the nick of time."

Ashley nodded. Then she sat down with Ariel in her lap and they hugged each other, Ashley whispering, "Grandpa's gonna be all right. See? Everything's going to be all right." Ariel was crying harder and harder, pressing herself into her mom's embrace.

I touched Ashley's shoulder. "I'll get you those drinks now."

One end of the corridor ended in a door with a red sign that said, "Authorized personnel only." I passed a corridor branching off from ours. Then another. Finally, to the left, a doorway led to a kitchenette and vending machines.

I stopped in the doorway. A woman stood in the room feeding coins into the coffee machine. My heart seized, and I nearly gasped.

Even from the back, I recognized her gray hair, her slumped shoulders. It was Marina. She wore a white shawl, pulled tight around her, as if she were cold.

She picked her last coin from her open palm and dropped it into the machine. She pressed a button. The machine beeped.

"No," she whimpered, pressing the button again and again.

It simply beeped more.

Then she spun around, turning from the machine, and I ducked back into the hallway. An instant later, she emerged from the room and turned left. She didn't see me as she hurried down the hallway and then turned into a room at the far end.

By the kitchenette, the vending machine blinked. Apparently, Marina had run out of coins. She was just a dollar shy of what she needed for a coffee.

I fed the machine to get a coffee and then got a bottled

water. Then headed back out into the hallway, eager to get back to Ashley and Ariel.

But I stopped and looked over my shoulder. For a long while, I stood still, feeling the tug of the Waterstons from one end of the corridor and of Marina Kemp from the other. The coffee cup in my hand radiated warmth. The cold bottle promised fresh, fine water.

I made a decision.

I turned and headed down the hallway. At the end, I found Marina sitting by her mother's bedside. The machines monitoring Ophelia's ebbing life beeped. The old woman lay motionless, eyes closed, mouth open under an oxygen mask, her breath coming with a steady, artificial rhythm.

Beyond her, a bank of windows looked out on the parking lot and the shadowy trees beyond. But among the distant mountains, the black sky was turning a dark blue. Night was slowly relinquishing its grip, surrendering to day.

Marina looked up. Her eyes were bloodshot. Exhausted.

Even so, a flicker of surprise passed over her face.

I handed her the cup of coffee and bottled water.

"This is for you," I said.

She received the drinks in silence. She simply stared at me with profound confusion. I gave a single nod, and reaching out, touched her shoulder. A gentle touch.

"I—" she said, barely a whisper.

"I understand," I said.

I turned and headed back out—back to the vending machines to get drinks for Ashley and Ariel. But as I reached the doorway, Marina called my name.

"Thank you," she said. "For understanding."

Then I left her, confident that I had done what I could. For now.

26

"I don't believe he would kill himself," I told Mom, as we rode down the elevator at Holloway Hospital.

"I don't either," Mom said. "But belief is one thing. Evidence is another. The suicide note was written on a typewriter at the Waterstons. Barry's own. He's old-school like your dad. The pills were Ashley's. Prescription. Eye witnesses put Barry at the scene of the crime at the right time. And finally, he's got a compelling motive."

I shook my head. It still didn't make sense to me.

The elevator pinged, and the doors opened. We strode through the hospital lobby and out the revolving doors to the parking lot. Beyond the trees, the horizon had transformed from dark to powder blue with a bloom of lilac.

"Something's fishy about all this," I said as we crossed the parking lot, heading for Mom's cruiser. "If Barry wanted to commit suicide, would he do it at the kitchen table, where his granddaughter might find him? I don't think he'd put her through that. And why leave his snack half-eaten? He left the pickle untouched."

"A pickle doesn't prove anything. Suicide isn't a rational thing."

"That's the thing, though. In this case, it ought to be. He murdered Ralph and then realized he was going to get caught. So he decides to escape—or pay for his crimes—by taking a bunch of pills. He leaves a note telling us he's sorry. That's highly rational."

Mom nodded. "It does have the appearance of rationality."

"Plus," I said. "The back door..."

I opened the door to the passenger side, and in that moment, glanced up at the hospital. Among all the windows in the big building—dozens and dozens of them—my eyes caught a flash of white and zeroed in on it immediately.

A woman wearing a white shawl was standing at the window, apparently gazing up at the sky. The window cracked open. But the room was dark and her face, even most of her body, remained in shadow. It was the shawl that stood out.

Marina's white shawl. Impossible to miss.

A shock made me jump back from the car, like electricity jolting me, and I let out a sound.

It startled Mom.

"Park," she said. "Are you all right?"

"The white shawl," I said, a grin dawning on my face. "The white shawl and the red scarf. Both so impossible to miss."

Mom stared at me. "Park, you're going to have to explain that."

And I did. And soon, Mom was grinning, too.

27

An opulent breakfast decorated the long table in the Gilder mansion's garden. Three-tiered silver trays held miniature cakes. Each place setting included crystal bowls with yoghurt and fruit. Mrs. Gilder sat upright in her chair, holding a fork. A piece of mango speared and suspended in the air. But she didn't appear about to eat—she simply held it and stared at us.

"Chief Lee," she barked. "I'm not accustomed to such intrusions. I trust it means you have urgent business with me."

Mom, brisk and business-like, stepped down to the lawn. I followed her. Deputy Douglas positioned himself by the door. Across from the butler, Dave, who gave the deputy a look. Wary. Watchful.

"Urgent," Mom said to Mrs. Gilder, "and important."

Mrs. Gilder put down her fork. "I'm listening."

Eric took a sip of coffee and raised his eyebrows at his wife. Iris shrugged and dabbed at her mouth with her napkin.

She said, "No offense to Parker, but do we want a journalist present?"

"Parker stays," Mom said. "In fact, I'll let her explain."

Mrs. Gilder waved a hand with a kind of regal impatience. "Go ahead, then. Enlighten us with your urgent and important business."

I said, "Mrs. Gilder, we know who murdered your son and why."

Mrs. Gilder stiffened. She pushed herself away from the table, so she sat straight—as rigid as a board—against the chair back.

I continued. "When your son Ralph returned to Allington, he came for a single purpose: to get more money. We can't know whether he planned to stay. My guess is that he didn't."

"Yet he didn't come to me for money," Mrs. Gilder said. "I would've given it to him."

"Presumably, he worried you'd convince him to stay. According to what he told Ashley, you'd convinced him before."

In my mind, I thought *coerced*, but I was sure Mrs. Gilder wouldn't react well to such a strong word.

"Or Ralph felt guilty," I added.

Eric snorted. "Unlikely."

"Of course," I said, turning to Eric with a nod, "there was probably also another reason. Like he didn't want to risk bumping into his older brother. He knew there'd be a confrontation. Potentially a dangerous one."

Eric sighed. "You guess. You suppose. What kind of investigation is this? And why is a journalist talking? Chief Lee, I'd like to hear from you."

"Eric," Iris said, resting a hand on his arm and stroking it. "Let's give them a chance. We've been cooperative throughout this ordeal, and we've got nothing to hide." Was her hand trembling a little? She caught me looking at it and shoved it under the table. Then met my gaze. "Please—go ahead, Parker."

"Ralph even returned to Allington under a different name," I continued. "Rolf Goldman. But why bother with such an elaborate ruse?"

Iris said, "Well, presumably the police in half a dozen states were looking for him. Considering what he did for a living."

I shook my head. "Nell Shamus was the only one who'd connected the dots. Local police all knew Ralph under his various pseudonyms. No, Ralph tried to keep his visit a secret because he feared discovery from someone here in Allington. He visited Ashley, hoping to get some money out of her. He got lucky. Barry, her dad, offered to pay him to stay away. A day later, Barry even went to Ralph's room to deliver the cash, leaving wet boot prints in the hallway. But by then, Ralph was dead and didn't answer the door."

"Or he went through the door and killed my brother," Eric interrupted. "Look, I've heard enough. Once again, *The Gazette* is speculating and throwing dirt at respectable families. It's time our butler showed you the door."

"Eric," Mrs. Gilder snapped. "Let her speak."

Iris nudged her husband, giving him an insistent look, and Eric's frown deepened. He whispered something to her about needing to defend themselves, and how "playing nice" would only get them so far. She shushed him.

I continued: "At night, the killer, with help from an accomplice, moved the body out of room 9. They got it into a boat. A guest heard something and, looking out, thought a burglar—or maybe only a fisherman—was lurking on the dock. A close call for the pair on the dock. After that, the killer and his accomplice rowed to the island and dumped the body. They hid it well. It might have taken days—or even weeks or months—before someone found him."

I paused, looking from one person to the next. "But then my mom started asking everyone in town about an intruder —a possible burglar—who'd tried to break into room 9 at the inn. The killer saw an opportunity. What if the police became convinced that the burglar had murdered Ralph? That would be ideal."

"In fact," Mom said, "we were thinking along those lines."

I continued: "So the killer returned to the island, perhaps with his accomplice, to bring the body out into the open. To stage it. Because now he wanted Ralph to be discovered as soon as possible, so the police would connect the mysterious burglar to the death. It was so important, in fact, that the killer put a red scarf around Ralph's neck. When I spotted it from the air, I didn't stop to think about how odd the scarf was. Not even later, when Nell Shamus told us that Ralph wore inconspicuous clothes. Jeans. T-shirts. Simple button-downs. Nothing that would draw attention to himself. So what in the world was he doing wearing a bright red scarf?"

"Who knows what went through his crazy head?" Eric said. "A man who pretends to be a pastor, so he can steal money from poor, innocent people, doesn't think like a normal human being."

"Shut up," Mrs. Gilder snapped.

Iris flinched, as if she absorbed the attack more than her husband. Eric just became more morose. He stabbed the food on his plate with his fork, but didn't eat.

"But the red scarf wouldn't work on its own," I continued. "Someone had to see it. And what's the best way to spot a dead body wearing a bright red scarf? Why, from the air, of course."

A clatter of silverware.

"That's outrageous," Eric said, getting to his feet. "This is slander. Clear and simple. I want you to know that—"

"Sit down, Eric," Mrs. Gilder said. Cool as ice. "Now."

Her son stared at her. "But Mom..."

"Sit—" She stared back. Dead eyes. "—down."

Then, as Eric sank back down to his chair, she gestured for me to carry on.

"Given the stories we run in *The Gazette*," I continued, "it was easy enough for you to make a call, Eric, and gush about a new aerial tour. The next morning, I was high in the air, perfectly positioned to discover the body. Now, the cops would think Ralph died out there. Which was important, since the staff at the Lakeview Inn had seen you on the day of the murder. Iris was looking at rooms for her dad's visit, which was a fabrication, of course. But since the murder supposedly happened on Gull Island, your presence at the inn that afternoon wasn't suspicious."

Mom said, "But then forensics showed Ralph died in room 9."

"Yes, that complicated your plans," I told Eric. "But you had a card up your sleeve. Barry Waterston. He was doing work at Allington Tours' offices, and, in fact, he was the one who told you about your brother's return in the first place. And about the payoff. That made you realize Barry had a motive. Plus, the payoff gave him an opportunity to kill Ralph. Now, if the authorities were led to believe Barry was the killer..."

Mrs. Gilder was staring at Eric. Her voice came out hushed. Almost a whisper. "You did this. You killed Ralph."

"He was rotten to the core," Eric growled, flinging his

fork onto the table. "And despite this, you wanted him to come home. He'd bleed the business dry. He'd steal everything he could carry and then run off to some corner of the country where he couldn't be found. I couldn't let him do that."

"Eric," Iris said, pleading, tugging at his sleeve. "Please. You don't need to say anything."

He tore free from her. But said nothing.

"And you," Mrs. Gilder said, narrowing her eyes at Iris. "You helped Eric murder Ralph. You put my dead son on that boat of yours."

"We were trying to do what was right," Iris said, her shoulders shaking with sobs. "We were trying to protect our family."

I could go on detailing the case, but I didn't need to. The truth was out in the open. Mom motioned for Deputy Douglas to join us. "Deputy, please cuff the two of them and read them their rights."

Deputy Douglas rounded the table and got out a pair of handcuffs. As he cuffed Iris, tears streamed down her face. Then he cuffed Eric, who stood straight-backed with a stoic glare on his face. Neither fought.

As Deputy Douglas escorted the two culprits past Mrs. Gilder, Eric turned to his mom and said, "You taught me to do everything for this family. And anything necessary. So I did."

Then he walked on. Mom and Deputy Douglas led Eric and Iris Gilder out of the garden. Dave, the butler, stood with wide eyes, shoulders slumped, clearly uncertain about what to do.

I lingered for a moment, watching Mrs. Gilder.

She got up. Unsteady. Arms and legs shaking. A hand

reaching out for balance. She wobbled on her feet and I rushed forward to catch her.

But she pushed my hands aside.

"Hands off," she snapped. "I don't need your help. I don't need anybody's help."

She squared her jaw and glared at the empty table.

"The fools. I was never going to give half the business to Ralph. As if I didn't know my own son. Ralph couldn't handle it. Like he couldn't handle being a father." She shook her head. "No, I wanted him to come home because he belonged here. A family belongs together."

She stared at the table. A table surrounded by empty chairs.

"A family belongs together..." she muttered.

28

T hat Sunday, like every Sunday, we gathered at Shepherd's Gate Church for Amy's sermon: Mom, Dad, Ray, Scottie, Joy, and me.

Amy read from the Gospel of Matthew.

"You have heard that it was said, 'Love your neighbor and hate your enemy.' But I tell you, love your enemies and pray for those who persecute you, that you may be children of your Father in heaven."

She looked out over the congregation.

"Jesus took the idea of loving your neighbor and expanded it to include loving your enemy. Well, sometimes we need a reminder that the first principle still stands. Love your neighbor. It can be difficult. It can even be difficult to love our own family. Much easier to judge them, and so tempting to act as judge, jury, and executioner."

I glanced over at Mom, who was sitting in the same pew as me. She looked over at me, a serious look on her face. We were both thinking of the Gilders—and so, it seemed, was Amy. In fact, most people in the congregation would make the connection, since everyone knew by now that Eric and Iris Gilder had been arrested for the murder of Ralph Gilder and the attempted murder of Barry Waterston.

Amy continued: "It's as we read in Romans, 'let us stop passing judgment on one another. Instead, make up your mind not to put any stumbling block or obstacle in the way of a brother or sister.' Life is full of suffering. God gave us this life to bring more love to each other, not more suffering." She smiled at the congregation. "Now, let us pray."

After the sermon was over, we gathered for coffee and cake. Many people lingered. As Dad said, "It was a zinger of a sermon. Plus, there's a lot of gossip to catch up on."

As usual, Joy provided coffee, tea, and juice, as well as a selection of cakes and cookies from Cafe Larke. I ate an oatmeal-and-raisin cookie.

"Try the brownies," Scottie said, his mouth full of a chocolaty mass. "They're delicious."

"I bet they are," I said. "But sometimes I feel like oatmeal and raisin."

"Like rainy days," Roxie said. "I love summer and sunshine, but sometimes I crave a cozy, drizzly day."

"Amen," Dad said, who was all about cozy, drizzly days.

Nearby, I saw Amy talking to Marina Kemp. Amy was smiling and spoke with animation, while Marina looked awkwardly down at her feet and nodded. I joined them, bringing an oatmeal cookie and a cup of coffee for Marina.

"Marina," I said, handing her the coffee and cookie. "I'm so sorry for your loss."

"Thank you," she said, her voice empty of vitality. Completely drained. She took a sip of coffee and nibbled the cookie.

"Park," Amy said. "You'll never believe it. It's about the donations. Marina just showed me."

"We got a lot at Thursday night's event?" I said.

"Yes—that, too. But sometime Friday or yesterday, someone stuffed the donation box full of cash. They must've come in while the church was open, but when I wasn't around. And the crazy thing is that it's exactly what we need to reach and even exceed our goals for the fundraiser."

"That is crazy," I agreed.

"I told Marina that it's as if someone—" She glanced upward. "—helped us a little."

I looked at Mariana. She was studying her coffee intently.

"Nothing like getting a helping hand when you need it," I agreed, riffing on Amy's idea.

Marina gave a slight nod. Amy cocked her head, watching her, a look of sympathy on her face.

"Come, Marina," Amy then said, gently now. "Tell me again about your wonderful mother, Ophelia. How did she teach you to knit and cook at such a young age?"

They wandered off, heads bowed low. Amy would help Marina through her grief. It was her superpower. She knew when to bring a person into the present moment or when to talk about the past.

For my own part, I'd abandoned my attempt to expose the truth. Instead, I'd prioritized my sympathy for Marina, and that had cleared up the mystery of the missing money. Yes, she might've spent some of it on her mom's medical bills, but she'd returned the rest, and now she would, no doubt, continue to donate hours and hours of her hard work to the church and other institutions.

"A helping hand, huh?" Dad said, coming up behind me. He'd clearly been eavesdropping on my conversation with

Amy and Marina. He took a sip of coffee. Then winked at me. "You almost sound as if you know something about that helping hand."

"I almost do. But not enough to write a story."

He put an arm around me. "That's my girl."

THANK YOU for reading this Parker Lee Mystery.

Want a **free short story**? Sign up for my newsletter to hear when the next book comes out and I'll share the story with you:

https://mpblackbooks.com/newsletter/

If you enjoyed this book, please take a moment to **leave a review online.** It makes it easier for other readers to find the book. Thanks so much!

And while you wait for the next Parker Lee mystery, turn the page for a preview of *The Soggy Cannoli Murder*, book 1 in an Italian-American Cozy Mystery Series.

29

EXCERPT FROM THE SOGGY CANNOLI MURDER

"You got a death wish?"

Mark Lewis, owner of Cafe Roma, shouldered me aside. He grabbed the portafilter handle out of my hand and yanked it from the espresso machine. Then he knocked the coffee back into the bucket with fresh grounds and quickly refilled it, tamping down one shot instead of two. Standing this close to him, I caught a whiff of alcohol off his breath.

"I told you, one shot of espresso per coffee."

"But the woman ordered an Americano," I said, keeping my voice low since the woman in question stood only a few feet away at the cafe counter waiting for her coffee. "She'll need two shots of espresso."

"She'll get one," he said.

He ran the ancient espresso machine. It roared and shook as one shot of ink-black coffee splashed into the white ceramic cup. Then Mark added hot water from the wand until it threatened to spill over the rim.

I watched with a mix of amazement and horror. The Americano was so watery, I could see the bottom through the murky liquid. You'd be forgiven if you thought it was a cup of tea.

"That's not an Americano," I said. "That's water with a whisper of coffee."

"If you want to waste your own money, that's fine. But don't waste mine. There's about 32 shots of espresso to a pound of coffee beans. Cut that in half and I can make my current inventory last another three months."

I was confused. "What happens in three months?"

"Nothing," he snapped. "The point is, I'm not in the business of giving my money away to customers. *Capisce*?"

This wasn't the first time this morning that Mark had peppered his speech with Italian. He was about as Italian as the Mayflower. But apparently it was part of his act—after all, Cafe Roma, like the entire town of Carmine, was supposed to be quintessentially Italian-American.

He stood back and folded his arms across his chest, eyeing me critically.

"Do you want this job or not?"

I bit my lip. Mark Lewis was a terrible boss and his cafe was a disaster. The espresso machine coughed up coffee as if it were dying. Mold spread across the ceiling. Water damage had warped and cracked the laminate floors, making more than one customer wrinkle their nose and turn away at the door.

And yes, my number one wish was to work here.

I nodded.

"Well, this job interview isn't over yet," he said, a gleam in his eye. He seemed to enjoy watching me squirm. He picked up the cup and handed it to me, and none too gently, either. Coffee sloshed over the edges.

"Here," he said. "Go serve her."

"*Va bene*, boss," I mumbled, and his eyes narrowed.

"*Va* what?"

I figured that if he could serve up Italian phrases, so could I. Though I might have sprinkled it with a little too much sarcasm.

In my defense, it was hard to get on board with the fake tribute to Italy that was Cafe Roma's bread and butter. But that was where the money was, according to Mark. New Yorkers, in particular, loved it. Carmine was called the "Little Italy" of New Jersey's distant Wessex County, and if out-of-towners bothered to come this far, it was to indulge in Italian-American culture.

As I went back to serving the customer, Mark settled down on a chair in the corner—hidden from customer view by the bulky, rust-fringed espresso machine—and picked up a dog-eared paperback, a chunk of its cover ripped off at the bottom. It was entitled *A Moron's Step-by-Step Guide to Living with Less.*

Somehow, it wasn't a surprising reading choice given his stinginess.

The gray-haired woman who had ordered the Americano had also asked for a cannoli. I slid the coffee cup and plate with the pastry toward her. She eyed both coffee and cannoli with suspicion, and frankly, so did I.

The cannoli had recently been wrapped in plastic and deep frozen, but the microwave in the cafe's back-room kitchen had remedied that. It was so soggy that it had deflated and half melted onto the plate.

The woman sighed, but she laid a wrinkled 5-dollar bill on the counter, the price of the coffee and cannoli special. Then grabbed her coffee cup and plate and found a seat by the window. In a moment, she was engrossed in a newspaper.

I checked the time on my phone. It was 11 am, three

hours after the cafe's regular opening time. Apart from the window seats running along the left-hand side, where the woman sat, the long, narrow cafe had four tiny tables pressed up against the right-hand wall. They were empty. The woman was the only customer.

The woman had chosen the best spot at the cafe's wall-length windows. Beyond where the woman sat, I got a good view of Garibaldi Avenue, Carmine's main drag, as well as Poplar Street, which ran down along Cafe Roma.

I leaned on the counter, staring out at the small town that was supposed to be my new home. It was Monday morning. Cars drifted up and down Garibaldi and people wandered to work or rushed to take care of morning errands.

On the opposite corner of Poplar and Garibaldi, a woman came out of Parisi & Parisi, Attorneys at Law, and pulled up the rolling steel shutters, opening for business. A bright yellow bicycle whizzed past. All down the street, bunting stretched from lamp post to lamp post, festooning Garibaldi Avenue with small Italian and U.S. flags.

I wondered if this place would ever feel like home, if I'd ever feel settled again.

"Excuse me."

The gray-haired woman interrupted my thoughts. She approached the counter, carrying the coffee cup and the plate. She set them both down with a grimace.

"I'm sorry, but I simply must speak up."

She made it sound like she was doing her civic duty. Guessing what she'd complain about, I didn't disagree.

"This Americano is so weak, it hardly tastes like coffee, and honestly, you should be ashamed of this cannoli. It's nothing like the photos you advertise outside." She gestured toward the sidewalk sign outside the cafe entrance. "If I didn't know better, I'd think this was a frozen cannoli that had been heated in a microwave. I can't eat this."

I apologized profusely, feeling the very shame she'd told me I ought to feel—multiplied by ten. There was right and there was wrong, and false advertising was squarely in the "wrong" category. I offered to get her another baked good and a fresh cup of coffee.

"Never mind the pastry," she said. "Coffee's all I want."

I removed her cup and the plate with the half-eaten cannoli, and I turned to make a fresh Americano.

Mark lowered his paperback. He placed a folded sheet of legal paper into the book to mark his place and glared at me.

"What do you think you're doing?"

"I'm making that woman another cup of coffee."

"Did she pay for another?"

"No, but—"

"Then why is she getting another? Is Cafe Roma a charity?"

"This coffee"—I stubbornly stood my ground—"is too weak. The cannolis you serve are soggy. And if we want customers to come back, we'll need to make sure they like the food and drinks, right?"

Mark gave me a long, hard glare. It seemed to be his favorite form of communication, and I guessed he'd had years of practice.

It did not make him attractive.

The crazy thing was that under different circumstances, he would have been a handsome forty-something-year-old. He had a finely cut jaw and a pair of arresting green eyes that would have made a casting agent look twice at him. But despite my Hollywood experience, or maybe because of it, I believed people's faces meant less than their hearts. Mark could have been a supermodel and his personality would still make him ugly.

Finally, when he thought his glare had done its damage, he said, "If she won't pay for the coffee, then you will."

"Wait, what?"

"You heard me, Bernie. The woman can pay for another coffee if she wants it. Or you can fork out the money. I sure as hell won't cover it."

"But—"

I stopped myself. *Drop it*, I thought. *It was your pigheaded belief in right or wrong that landed you in this mess in the first place. And this town.*

"Your resume, assuming it's true, says you're an experienced barista."

He pulled the folded piece of paper from his shirt pocket and opened it. Through the paper, I could see my name at the top, the false one I'd been given: Bernie Smyth.

"Even if you lied about your experience, you'd better start acting like one. Think you can do that?"

"I can do that," I said through gritted teeth.

Because yes, indeed, I could act.

He returned to reading his book, mumbling something about paying too much in wages. He pulled open the cupboard beneath the espresso machine and produced a small metal hip flask, which he took a swig from.

That explained why he reeked of alcohol.

I returned my attention to the customer and her fresh cup of coffee.

My experience as a barista wasn't entirely untrue, though admittedly a little "amplified" on my resume. Before I had my breakthrough as an actress, I worked at a coffee van in Los Angeles. It was a simple little truck, with only three drinks on offer: Americano, cappuccino, and latte.

Even leaving aside that bit of experience, I knew what a good cup of coffee ought to taste like. I had standards.

And I could be pretty stubborn about those standards.

So I made the gray-haired woman an Americano the way I'd learned to: two shots of espresso and hot water, the crema coating the surface. It felt good to make the coffee the way it ought to be made, and when the woman picked up the cup and took a sip and smiled, her joy warmed my insides.

"Ah," she said. "Much better, thanks."

We smiled at each other and I thought, *Hey, maybe this gig will work out after all.*

As the woman returned to her seat by the window, I saw she'd left her newspaper on the counter. I was about to call out to her, when a jolt, like electric shock, shot through me.

The newspaper had been folded to the front of the Entertainment section and there, in a large photo spanning the page, was my face. The headline said, "Death of America's Top TV Show Silver & Gold: Jay Casanova in prison, Bernadette Kovac STILL missing."

They'd picked a promotional photo from the last season of *Silver & Gold*. My character, Eve Silver, was standing back to back with Adam Gold, played by Jay Casanova. It was a shock to see him. I had avoided the news since the big trial, and the last time I saw him, he had been screaming at me across the courtroom as guards handcuffed him: "I'll get you for this, Bernadette—you'll regret your lies."

They hauled him off to prison while a team of U.S. Marshalls whisked me away, an unexpected end to America's most popular TV show, not to mention my acting career.

"Junk," Mark said, and I jumped. "TV these days is nothing but trash."

He leaned over and jabbed a finger at the photo.

"No one will miss that show any more than they'll miss those rotten actors."

I hoped he was right. If nobody missed the stars of *Silver & Gold*, then they also wouldn't notice the similarities between Bernadette Kovac and Bernie Smyth. I wore my hair short now, and my natural color—raven black—was strikingly different from Eve Silver's blonde curls. Besides, who would guess that Bernie Smyth, working a minimum wage job at a cafe in New Jersey, had anything to do with the famous actress?

Mark glared at the photo in the newspaper, picking it up for a closer look.

"What else have I seen that actress in? A movie? She looks familiar..."

My heart beat faster.

"She used to be everywhere. You've probably seen her in magazines and in ads and in TV commercials..."

"I guess so..."

He continued to study the photo.

Then, abruptly, he threw the paper down.

"All right, Bernie Smyth. You've got the job."

He held out a keychain with two keys.

My heart did a little somersault. "What? I do?"

"If you still want it."

"I do, I do."

I took the keychain. He explained one was the key to the front, the other to the back. Later, he'd show me where to put the garbage in the back alley.

He looked at his wristwatch. "Right now, I'm going out for lunch. You keep an eye on things."

I nodded, hardly able to absorb the good news. I got a job. This was a big step toward finding some kind of stability, while also keeping my identity a secret.

"I'll be back in an hour or two," Mark said.

But before he left, he cast another frown at the newspaper on the counter.

"Hmm..."

He grabbed a pen that lay on the cash register and he drew a large circle around Eve Silver's face. Next to it, he put a question mark: "?"

"I'm sure I'll remember where I've seen her."

I nodded mechanically, no words coming out. My mouth had gone dry. If he did remember, I was in deep trouble.

Want more? Grab *The Soggy Cannoli Murder* at your favorite online bookstore.

MORE BY M.P. BLACK

A Wonderland Books Cozy Mystery Series

A Bookshop to Die For

A Theater to Die For

A Halloween to Die For

A Christmas to Die For

A Yarn Shop to Die For

A Hair Salon to Die For

An Italian-American Cozy Mystery Series

The Soggy Cannoli Murder

Sambuca, Secrets, and Murder

Tastes Like Murder

Meatballs, Mafia, and Murder

Parker Lee Mystery Series

The Art of Murder

The Deadly Circle

Trouble Brewing

A Killer View

Short stories

The Italian Cream Cake Murder (FREE)

ABOUT THE AUTHOR

M.P. Black writes fun cozies with an emphasis on food, books, and travel—and, of course, a good old murder mystery.

Besides writing and publishing his own books, he helps others fulfill their author dreams too through courses and coaching.

M.P. Black has lived in many places, including Brooklyn, Vienna, and San Jose de Costa Rica. Today, he and his family live in Copenhagen, Denmark, where coziness ("hygge") is a national pastime.

Join M.P. Black's free newsletter to download a free story and get updates on books and special deals:

https://mpblackbooks.com/newsletter/